"Excuse me," said a deep voice beside me. "Mind if I sit down?"

I looked up and was astonished to see that Steve Blumenthal was pulling up a chair right next to mine. His blond hair was sleek, and his eyelashes were like a sort of dark smudge around eyes of clear gray. He was gorgeous, all right.

"Aren't you Corky's cousin Fran?" he asked.

For a second, I couldn't catch my breath. Here he was right beside me, the fabulous Steve Blumenthal, just as Corky had promised. And he'd actually spoken to me! This was the moment I had been waiting for.

"That's right," I answered. "I'm Fran."

Dear Reader:

Thank you for your continuing support of First Loves and your many helpful suggestions. Just as you have requested, we are now including mystery and suspense elements in our books. We are also publishing more stories with the same characters, and have added a new romantic suspense series by Becky Stuart, the Kellogg and Carey Stories. Look for *Journey's End,* the first of these, in October.

And check out our new covers. We have listened to you! From now on you will see that our heroes and heroines will look just like the characters in our books, and more like you and your friends.

Nancy Jackson
Senior Editor
FIRST LOVE FROM SILHOUETTE

SUGAR 'N' SPICE
Janice Harrell

First Love from Silhouette

Published by Silhouette Books New York

America's Publisher of Contemporary Romance

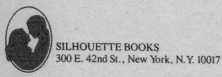
SILHOUETTE BOOKS
300 E. 42nd St., New York, N.Y. 10017

Copyright © 1985 by Janice Harrell

Distributed by Pocket Books

ISBN: 0-373-06159-5

First Silhouette Books printing October 1985

10 9 8 7 6 5 4 3 2 1

America's Publisher of Contemporary Romance

Printed in the U.S.A.

RL 6.3, IL Age 11 and up

First Loves by Janice Harrell

Puppy Love #67
Heavens to Bitsy #95
Secrets in the Garden #128
Killebrew's Daughter #134
Sugar 'n' Spice #159

JANICE HARRELL is the eldest of five children, and spent her high-school years in the small, central Florida town of Ocala. She earned her B.A. at Eckerd College and her M.A. and Ph.D. from the University of Florida. For a number of years she taught English at the college level. She now lives in Rocky Mount, North Carolina, with her husband and their young daughter.

Chapter One

Mom used to say that my first word was "no." That's an exaggeration, but I admit that I learned pretty early how to draw a firm line. It was only plain self-defense against some of the characters I had to deal with.

Take my Uncle Mark, for instance. I still remember the raccoon coat with matching hat he sent me. It was a lucky thing Mom didn't make me wear it. I can imagine the sensation I would have caused in the second grade if I'd shown up one day looking like a cross between Davy Crockett and a Mogwai. Another time he called me up all the way from Africa and asked if I wanted a live chimpanzee. Looking back, it's hard to believe he was serious, but I wouldn't have put it past him. In fact, I wouldn't have put it past him to ship me a piranha for the bathtub. With Uncle Mark you had to be quick to dig in your heels and say no or you'd end up with a whole zoo on your hands. Luckily, I didn't hear from him all that much. He was usually busy acting in a movie somewhere. But Corky, my cousin, lived only a few miles down the road and in a different way he was just as bad.

With Corky the danger wasn't that he was going to ship me a raccoon coat or a chimp. It was that he was going to end up persuading me to do some of the crazy things he did, so I would end up with six or eight broken bones. Some of my best practice in saying no came with him. He would say, "You wanna learn how to do a double backward somersault off the high dive, Fran?" Or "Hey, Fran, don't you think it'd be neat to try going over the falls in a barrel? It's not so far down and there are just a few rocks."

Since Corky spent so much time on horses himself, it was especially hard for him to understand that I didn't want to learn to ride. He was always saying things like "Just hop up on Devil, here…whoa, Devil, calm down, boy…come on, Fran, get up and I'll show you how to jump fences. Honest, it's a piece of cake."

The funny thing was that in spite of Corky's being the reckless kind, while I preferred to live out my natural life span in one piece, we hung around a lot together. Maybe that was because we had the same sense of humor, and we always agreed on who we liked and who we didn't. Whatever the reason was, Corky was just about my best friend.

To look at us, nobody would have guessed we were cousins. He looked like a young boxer at the top of his form—broad shoulders, a very flat stomach, and a nose that looked as if it had met with one fist too many, until you looked at his father and saw where he had inherited it from. He had dark, springy hair that wouldn't stay put and the kind of generally battered-looking face that would have never made a girl swoon unless she happened to notice his grin.

As for me, I was cut with a completely different cookie cutter. For one thing, I was totally nonathletic, and for another I have a kind of insipid prettiness that always guaranteed I'd be the kid picked for the part of Mary in the Christmas pageant. I remember when I was little, people cooed a lot over me. "Such a sweet-looking child," they would say. "She's got her father's eyes and her mother's soft blond hair." I'd feel smug then because I already saw that if it had gone the other way and I'd gotten Mom's eyes and Dad's hair, I would have ended up the only nearsighted, balding four-year-old in the neighborhood. I figured I'd had a narrow escape.

But all that was years ago. It had been a long time since I'd felt smug about my looks. I had gotten tired of people thinking I was sweet when I wasn't. The truth was, I had a habit of thinking the worst about everybody. I was your average, ordinary, uncooperative kid. In the fourth grade, Mrs. Melrose had even given me a C- on citizenship. But in spite of everything I could do, I ended up looking like the person you could trust to hold your ice cream cone and not lick it.

I was ready for a change. I felt as if I had come to a turning point in my life. Now that I was a sophomore, it was time for me to look like a person with an interesting past and not so much like Little Miss Sunbeam. It was time I went to some dances and had some real dates. I wanted to be taken seriously. I wanted Romance. That was why the coldest day in December found me curled up in front of the fire leafing through camp catalogues.

"What's this?" said Corky, picking up a catalogue with his free hand. His other one was holding one of Mom's chocolate chip cookies.

"A camp catalogue," I said.

"I can see that. I mean, what are you doing with a bunch of camp catalogues?" He glanced at the front cover. "You aren't a camper 'aged eight to twelve,' are you?"

I didn't want to tell Corky what I was planning to do because I had the feeling he was going to try to stop me. Still, he was going to have to find out sooner or later.

"I'm going to try to get a job as a camp counselor," I said.

He paled. "You mean you're thinking of going away for the summer?"

"That's right."

"But I'll be stuck here alone if you do. Tony's already got a job lined up in the mountains and Skip's spending the summer with his dad."

"There's always Rachel," I said.

"Very funny."

Rachel was Corky's on-again, off-again date. He often described her as having the best seat on a horse of any girl in Nash County, but even he had to admit she wasn't much good to talk to. The idea of having nobody but Rachel to pal around with all summer had completely wiped the carefree look off his face. I wrinkled my brow and concentrated hard on the page in front of me.

I noticed that Camp Winnehutchee had a fine-looking kitchen staff. A couple of the boys were really gorgeous. But how could I be sure those particular guys would be back this summer? Maybe I would be better off at Camp Kenshaw, which was coed and had a large staff of both boy and girl counselors all summer. Probably the thing to do would be to apply to several camps anyway, not just my first choice. That way, even if I didn't get Camp Kenshaw, I'd have a better chance of at least getting something.

"It's a crazy idea," protested Corky. "You could earn more money working for Mom doing the yard. Those places pay next to nothing. And what do you have there that you don't have right here at home?"

I did not usually discuss such matters with Corky, but the time had come to be blunt. "Boys," I said, looking back at the catalogue I was reading.

"So what am I?" he yelped.

"I don't mean boys that I shared the same playpen with," I said. "I mean boys that are good for romance."

"We didn't share the same playpen," he muttered.

He really was against my going, but I had no intention of letting him change my mind. This was where my practice in digging in my heels would come in handy. I was going to have to be firm. I knew that if I kept spending my summers in Wessconnett, the most exciting thing that was going to happen to me was edging Aunt Myra's vegetable garden. I had to be realistic. Not only did I have no social life in Wessconnett, but there was no hope things would get any better. I needed to get out of town and look for greener pastures. Camp Winnehutchee, I thought, here I come.

"I can get a guy for you," Corky said suddenly.

Against my better judgment I looked up at him. "How?"

He waved the question away. "Don't worry about that," he said. "Trust me."

That was when I should have said, "No, thank you," the way I usually did and just gone right back to reading about Camp Winnehutchee, but already I found myself weakening. Corky's proposal had its appeal. I knew my camp idea had drawbacks. For one thing I wasn't sure how good I would be at taking charge of a cabin full of eight-year-olds. I hadn't had much practice with kids. And another thing was I couldn't be absolutely sure of getting a camp job. I had noticed that in each catalogue they had a list of activities to be taught by the counselors, and the only thing I had been able to find on the lists that I was any good at was Frisbee throwing. It was a cinch I wasn't going to be able to teach the kids mountain climbing or (shudder) horseback riding. Maybe I should snap up Corky's offer, I thought. I'd seen him pull off tougher things. Maybe he could manage this boy thing, too, even though I didn't see how.

"A good boy?" I asked cautiously. "Somebody I'm going to like?"

"Sure," he said. "Trust me. By June first I promise to deliver, in good condition, one boy to Fran Delacorte. Scout's honor." He crossed his heart.

I thought about it. "Why can't you get the boy for me now? Why do I have to wait for June?"

"It may take me a while to work out the details," he said.

I could see that Corky didn't have the faintest idea how he was going to deliver on the promise. I hesitated a minute, trying to weigh my chances of getting a job at a summer camp against the chances that Corky would be able to come up with a really neat boy for me. After some careful thought, I decided that the odds were a little better with Corky. He had his little faults, but as far as I could remember he'd never yet failed to deliver on a solemn promise.

"Okay," I said.

He grinned and we clasped hands to signify the bargain was set.

As the school year wore on, I thought about our bargain a lot. But it was only when really warm weather began that I started to get nervous. Once it got to be late May it was too late to get any out of town job. Besides, I had already signed on with Aunt Myra to spend the summer keeping the vegetable garden and the lawn around the house in shape so she and Corky could give the endless horseback riding lessons that it took to keep the horses in oats. Now here I was already changing the spark plug in the lawnmower and sharpening my pruning shears for the summer, but still there was no sign of the boy Corky had promised me.

I decided it was time to bring up the subject.

"Corky," I said. "Do you remember the bargain we made?"

"Uh, sure," he said. "About getting a guy for you." He was about to give Devil a bath and was lining up various brushes.

"Could you tell me what you've got in mind?" I asked.

He grinned. "Sure thing," he said. "What do you think of Steve Blumenthal?"

I almost dropped my pruning shears. The idea took my breath away. "Steve Blumenthal? The new boy?" I said weakly.

"Right."

Steve Blumenthal was only the most gorgeous guy ever to darken the doors of Wessconnett High. I hadn't gotten to know him yet, but I had seen him in class. He had smooth blond hair, long eyelashes as soft-looking as a bee's wing, and a profile that was positively noble. There was no other word for it. When you saw him carrying his books past you into algebra class you just naturally thought of astronauts conquering space, of Alexander the Great, of Byron swimming the Hellespont. It didn't seem right that a guy who looked like Steve was wasting his time on algebra problems.

Corky looked at me wryly. "You like the idea, huh?"

"He'll do," I managed to say. "But what makes you think he would be interested in me?"

Corky trained the hose on the big horse, and the water hissed and streamed down its flanks. "Why not? Give yourself a little credit. Besides, I happen to know he's lonely. And point two, not to be disgustingly modest about it—he looks up to me. I think I can toss him your way. I have a certain amount of influence there."

"I didn't even know you knew him."

"He's been taking lessons from me Thursdays."

I imagined Steve up on a horse, his magnificent profile turned toward the sunset. It would be just like the last reel on an old-fashioned western.

"He bounces all over the place," said Corky, "so I have to put him on Boss. She'll put up with anything."

I was not interested in Corky's critique of Steve as a rider. "When do I get to meet him?" I said.

"Saturday, at the horse show. It's all set up. Just make sure you're there. At the supper break I'll ask you and Steve to go for a pizza with Rachel and me. You take it from there.''

Suddenly the idea of sharing a pizza with Steve Blumenthal made my stomach feel definitely unsteady. Also I wasn't sure what Corky meant by "take it from there." What were the two of us going to talk about? I had never even met him.

"What if he doesn't like me?" I said.

"Why shouldn't he like you? Besides, he hardly knows anybody yet, and I've already softened him up for you."

I began to feel a little better. Yeah, I thought. Why shouldn't he like me? I stared at Aunt Myra's vegetable garden almost in a trance. Aunt Myra and Uncle Joe's farm, with the stables, the broad lawn, and the fields of soybeans, sweet potatoes, and tobacco stretching in neat rows toward the horizon, was as ordinary and everyday as the palms of my hands. But now that Steve was about to enter my life suddenly it all seemed shiny and bright.

Corky laid the hose down on the cement and took a stiff brush to Devil's coat. "Maybe I should turn the hose on you next," he said crossly. "You look as if you're about to pass out."

"There's nothing wrong with me being interested in Steve," I said with dignity. "After all, you've got Rachel."

He snorted. I didn't quite hear every word he muttered, but he seemed to intend to convey that I'd never catch him getting all dopey about Rachel.

I went to hang the newly sharpened pruning shears up in the equipment barn, humming a little tune to myself. Then I got on my bike and headed home, still humming. Maybe this was going to be my lucky summer after all. Good old Corky. I knew I could count on him.

When I got home and stepped in the door, the kitchen had a wonderful smell of chocolate and fried chicken. Mom loves to cook, and she has the full figure of someone who always tastes the food as she goes. Her hair was frizzy from steam and there was a dab of cake flour on her chin, but she looked happy. I noticed the chocolatey smell was coming from a freshly iced cake on the counter. Mom smoothed her apron down over her round tummy, pulled a drumstick out of the frying pan, and laid it on a bed of paper towels to drain. "No calories, no cholesterol," she said. "This is magic fried chicken."

I perched on a stool near the stove. "Guess what?" I said. "Romance is about to enter my life."

Mom looked a little startled at first, but when I explained about Corky and me and Steve going out for pizza after the horse show, she went back to peacefully turning the chicken. "If Corky thinks this Steve is a nice boy," she said, "I'm sure he's fine."

"Steve is only the most beautiful boy in the school," I said. "He is so smooth I could practically eat him with a spoon."

"Then I hope you two hit it off," Mom said.

"Mom, who cares if I like him? Just looking at him is its own reward."

I reached over to the counter and sneaked a finger along the bottom of the cake to get some icing.

Just then I heard Dad at the front door, so I hopped down and went to get his slippers. He was on his feet most of the day at the cheese factory, and when he got home he liked to take off his shoes.

Most people don't think about how somebody has to make all those slices of cheese that go on bologna sandwiches, but the fact is, cheese is a big industry. Dad started out by studying dairy management in college. (That was the year Uncle Mark

ran away from home when he was only sixteen and ended up bumming around Aus-
tralia in a repertory company.) As soon as
Dad finished college he married Mom.
(Uncle Mark didn't make the wedding. That
was the year he was supporting himself by
singing on London street corners.) At first
Dad and Mom and I lived in Wisconsin,
home of cheese. But when I was in the first
grade Dad was able to come back to his old
home town and get a good job right in
Wessconnett's cheese factory.

As quality control supervisor of the
cheddar and processed cheese department
of the plant he had a lot of responsibility
and had to be always walking the floor taking plugs of cheese, testing, and making de-
cisions. He explained to me once that the
buying public didn't care much what the
cheese tasted like as long as it always tasted
exactly the same. That was why little things
like moisture control were really big deals at
the factory.

Just as I got the slippers under the table,
Dad came into the kitchen and tossed a
rolled-up magazine on the kitchen table. He
fell into a chair, grimaced, then pulled off
his shoes and groped for the slippers with
his stocking feet. "What a day," he
groaned. "Both Mankewitz and Bailey

called in sick, and on top of that we had to throw out the third batch.''

"What's that magazine?" asked Mom, glancing over at it.

"One of the guys brought it in," Dad said. "It's got Mark on the cover."

I looked over his shoulder. Sure enough, Uncle Mark had made the cover of *Personalities* with his new wife. She was Oriental and was wearing a necklace with a diamond pendant the size of an egg.

"Hmm," said Dad. "That new picture deal of Mark's must have been a humdinger."

The cover caption read, "Mark Delacorte's bride models his wedding gift to her—the Star of Delhi." Behind her, with his hands on her shoulders, stood Uncle Mark, looking majestically at the camera. It would have taken more than a beautiful young woman and the Star of Delhi to upstage a ham like Uncle Mark, and I wasn't surprised to find that in spite of all the competition he had, my eyes were drawn naturally to his face. I decided it would have taken a practiced eye to tell that Uncle Mark and Dad were brothers. The basic material they had been made of was the same, but Uncle Mark had all his teeth capped so they were an unbelievable pearly white, and he was never seen in public without his hairpiece, which made him look fifteen years younger than Dad right there. Maybe even more important was the difference in their expressions. Uncle Mark had arrogant-looking sleepy eyes, while Dad just looked friendly and as if his feet hurt.

"Mmm," said Dad suddenly. "Cake!" I noticed that the sight of the chocolate cake had temporarily revived him. I pecked him on the top of his head where the hair was getting thin.

"How do I rate that?" he said.

"I'm so glad you're not like Uncle Mark," I said.

"You just don't know him very well, kitten," Dad said. "Mark's okay."

Mom came over, wiping her hands on her apron, and looked at the magazine cover. "She looks very sweet," she said. "I do hope this one sticks."

"I wouldn't lay odds on it," I said as I leaned over to sneak another lick of chocolate icing. Really, the spectacle of Uncle Mark's dismal string of love affairs was enough to put a person off the idea of romance permanently. It was better not to dwell on it, I decided. Instead, I thought about Saturday and the horse show and

Steve. Beautiful, beautiful Steve whom Corky had promised to toss in my direction. I could hardly wait.

Chapter Two

When I got to the horse show Saturday, a glance at the ring showed me that I had got Dad to drop me off at about the right time. Several ponies were trotting around the ring pulling their drivers in little two-wheeled carts. I glanced at my program and saw this was Class 23, roadster ponies. I was going to be just in time for Corky's entry in Class 24, Morgan English Pleasure Horse. I pulled my folding yard chair over to a tree near the ring, where a crowd of people were already sharing what shade there was, and found myself a place to sit.

The Wessconnett horse show was nothing fancy. It was held on a part of the old Bailey farm leased by the pony club and had just the basics—a fenced riding ring, a judges' tent, and refreshment stand plus a large field filled with parked cars and horse trailers. Still, there was always a big turnout for the shows.

It was a pretty hot day, and I noticed some of the wilting spectators were trying to fan themselves with their programs. The ringmaster's voice, sounding hollow through the microphone, floated over us. "First place—Sonny's Jewel," he intoned, "driven by Gertrude Arness of Willow Run Stables, Hardyville." Sonny's Jewel, a high-stepping brown pony, wheeled around the ring pulling the shiny wood and leather cart behind him like a toy. There was scattered applause as he passed.

A moment later the ringmaster was asking for entries in the next class. "Morgan English Pleasure Horse," he called. I saw Corky riding Devil into the ring at the far end. Corky never looked his best in formal riding clothes. The neatness of the round bowler hat made his nose, by contrast, look more battered than ever. On top of that, today he looked as if his collar were too tight. If he was uncomfortable, though, he didn't let it affect his concentration. His face was as cool and intent as a monk's. The world around him might as well have not existed. He was only aware of the horse. A funnel cloud would have had to sweep the judges' tent away before he would have looked anywhere but straight ahead, between Devil's two ears.

Some good-looking Morgans followed him into the ring, but Devil had more class than any of them. When he twitched his flanks, his coat looked like satin rippling in sunshine. He was big for a Morgan, and the fierce look in his eye made him seem even bigger than he was. He snorted, making an ominous sound like a train coming through a tunnel, and I shivered a little, glad it was Corky up there on him and not me. Corky was always saying what a good horse Devil was, as long as you showed him who was boss, but since I had no hope at all of bossing Devil, that didn't encourage me a bit. I thought it was better to keep a distance between me and any high-strung animal weighing a ton or so.

"Excuse me," said a voice beside me.

I looked up and was astonished to see that Steve Blumenthal was pulling up a chair right next to mine. His blond hair was sleck, and his eyelashes were like a soft, dark smudge around eyes of clear gray. He was gorgeous, all right. "Aren't you Corky's cousin, Fran?" he asked. For a second I couldn't catch my breath. Here he was right next to me, the fabulous Steve Blumenthal! He had actually spoken to me! This was the moment I had been waiting for. "That's right," I said. "I'm Fran."

Then suddenly one of the red-headed Ferguson twins fell smack into Steve's lap, and we had to get the kid disentangled and set him on his feet to go back to chasing his brother. Steve surveyed the damage the twin's chocolate ice cream cone had done to his pants. "There's kind of a lot of confusion out here today, isn't there?" he said ruefully.

As he mopped ineffectively at the splotch of chocolate, I admired the beautiful neat line of his chin and his perfect nose. From far away I heard the ringmaster command "Trot, please."

A soft thump of hoofbeats on the turf of the ring and a fierce snort told me that Devil and Corky were riding by, so I pulled my eyes reluctantly away from Steve's beautifully chiseled profile and back to the ring. From where I was sitting, it looked as if Corky had Devil well in hand. The horse's head was arched high, and he was trotting so smoothly he looked as if he were floating.

"Isn't he terrific?" Steve said.

"He's a good horse," I admitted.

Steve shot me a reproachful look. "I mean Corky," he said.

"Oh, Corky always gets the best out of the horse," I said, blushing. I wanted so much to say just the right thing to Steve that it occurred to me maybe the safest thing would be to say nothing at all. Maybe I could stick to comments about the weather in the future.

As it turned out, the judging of the Morgans didn't take long because Devil just wiped the floor with those other suckers. He was far and away better than anything else in the ring. There was one slightly sticky moment when I was afraid he was going to blow the event by taking a bite out of the hide of the little gelding to his left, but by sheer force of will Corky kept him in line, and he came off looking like the sweetest-tempered horse that ever trod the ring.

"First place...Rosemere's Devil, ridden by Corky Hayden of Rosemere Stables, Wessconnett," said the ringmaster. The defeated horses filed out of the ring, and Corky and Devil trotted around the ring once in victory circuit. As they swept around to loud applause, Devil looked very pleased with himself. He was a thoroughly conceited horse.

Next came a short stirrup class for kids twelve and under. I saw a kid who couldn't have been more than four bouncing out into the ring on her pony. Riding enthusiasts waste no time getting their offspring down to business. I watched long enough to be sure that the four-year-old had a good chance of hanging on and wasn't likely to get trampled under the pony's hooves, then allowed my attention to wander back to Steve.

I cleared my throat. "Hot day," I said.

"It really is," he said with the surprised air of one who had only just happened to notice, now that it was pointed out to him, that it was almost ninety degrees in the shade. "Why don't we go get something to drink?" he said.

I felt a little thrill of pleasure. This was beginning to seem less like a chance meeting and more like a real social occasion. As I got up, I felt my skirt slowly coming unstuck from my legs. It really was hot.

We made our way through the stream of horses being led past the refreshment booth and took our places in the line. I noticed that Steve's shirt managed to look crisply pressed even while everyone else's outfits were damp and crumpled.

"I recognized you from Corky's description," he said.

I would have given a lot to know what Corky's description of me was, but I decided that on the whole it was better not to ask. It was all too likely that instead of saying, "My cousin Fran has eyes that haunt your dreams," he had said something like, "You can't miss her. She always forgets to shine her loafers."

Just then Corky came out of the judges' tent. He saw me standing with Steve and grinned in my direction. What with the people in line waiting for cold drinks and all the people riding by or leading horses to the ring, there was a lot of confusion, and I wasn't sure exactly what happened next, but I strongly suspect that the Ferguson twins had something to do with it. Suddenly, right behind me, a mare let out a frantic whinny and reared up. The child riding her, a little figure in a dusty bowler hat, slid immediately to the ground. There was another panicked whinny from the horse, and I was conscious of more hooves and legs flying around than I was perfectly comfortable with, but I put my arms around the little girl and pulled her away from the horse.

"Rebel," she wailed, lifting her tear-stained face.

Corky had made it to us in a flash. He grabbed the mare's reins. "I think she's hurt her leg," he said. The mare had quit rearing but was tossing her head and shuddering.

The little girl struggled to get away from me. "Rebel's hurt!" she shrieked, bursting into sobs. To my relief I saw a couple with the unmistakable look of parents running toward us. The hollow tones of the loudspeaker were already calling out, "Is there a vet present? If a vet is present, will he please come to the concession stand?"

I thankfully turned the little girl over to her parents. Luckily, when the vet appeared he judged the horse's injuries to be superficial and soon the little girl's hysterical sobs subsided.

An unexpected side effect of the accident was that the cold drink line thinned out as people rushed off to give eyewitness accounts of the accident to those who had missed it. Right away Steve I were able to move up a good bit in the line.

"Did you see that?" said Steve admiringly. "Corky had the horse under control in a second."

"He knows all about horses," I murmured.

Steve didn't seem to hear me. "That's what I want to be," he said with quiet radiance. "A hero."

I realized I didn't feel too comfortable with that statement, but after all, I told myself quickly, what could be more natural than his wanting to be a hero. He certainly looked like one. I had even noticed that myself. Probably he just wanted to deliver on the advertisement. But for the first time, the unworthy thought occurred to me that maybe Steve was a bit of a dope.

I guess my problem was that I wasn't the kind of person who believed in heroes. It might have had something to do with me having spent time since I was a kid watching Uncle Mark do his stuff on the screen. He looked great as the crime-fighting D.A., the death-defying space pilot, and the little man who took on Washington and won, but when the lights came on in the theater and you noticed the spilled popcorn on the floor, you realized it was really just silly old Uncle Mark up there.

I decided the best response to what Steve had said was to look at him sweetly and say nothing. I couldn't go wrong with that. So I collected my large cold drink at the concession counter, then gave him a sweet, shy look as we headed back toward our chairs. I noticed as we passed the Ferguson twins that they were sitting quietly in their chairs, looking strangely subdued. I would have loved to know what they had done to that horse.

Steve beamed at them. "Cute kids," he said.

Considering what one of them had just done to his pants leg, I thought this showed a noble and forgiving nature on his part, but I couldn't help noticing that he seemed to be a very trusting sort. Hadn't it occurred to him that it was odd for the Ferguson kids suddenly to look so quiet and well-behaved?

We found our places and sat down to watch the show, but we only had to sit through two more events. Then it was time for the supper break, and Corky showed up, Rachel in tow. His hair was plastered to his forehead in a couple of damp curls, but he had unbuttoned his shirt at the collar, abandoned his hat, and looked generally a lot more comfortable. Rachel, as usual, looked elegant in her riding habit with her hair in a bun. She had not only the deeply tanned face but also the impressive calm of a cigar store Indian.

"So you two found each other," said Corky. "What do you say we all go out for some pizza, huh? I'm starved." He glanced restlessly at his watch.

I knew Corky wanted to get moving because supper break was only a half hour, and he hated to miss even a single event at the show. At shows he invariably stuck to the ring like glue and stayed till the last pony and currycomb had been packed up.

"Terrific idea," said Steve. "Sounds great to me. What about you, Fran?"

"I'd like that," I said. Was it possible, I wondered, for anybody to be as enthusiastic about pizza as Steve?

We all got into Corky's little car. It only took a few minutes of me being squashed together with Steve in the cramped back seat to quiet any little qualms I had. What did I care if he was a little too trusting and idealistic for my taste? Just sitting next to him made my heart race and my palms feel moist.

I was surprised when Rachel twisted around in her seat to ask Steve a question because I had hardly ever heard her say anything that wasn't about horses. "Haven't I seen you out at the airport?" she said in her husky voice.

"That's right," said Steve. "I've got a job at the ticket counter for the summer."

"What a piece of luck!" I piped in. Wessconnett didn't have much of an airport, just a small one a bit past Corky's family's farm. It served a commuter airline and some private planes and was certainly no hub of glamor and excitement. Still, summer jobs of any kind were hard to find, and I was amazed Steve had managed to come up with one when he had only been in town a month.

"Not exactly luck," he admitted. "My dad manages the airport. I've been around planes all my life."

I wondered why I hadn't guessed that. Those gray eyes, those eaglelike good looks obviously belonged to a budding aviator. World War I flying ace—that was the role Steve was naturally cut out for. I imagined him climbing into his Sopwith Camel and pulling his goggles over his eyes. Naturally, he would raise his hand briefly in a debonair salute before he pulled on the throttle or whatever and disappeared into the thin blue of the sky, a gallant figure fighting against overwhelming odds. I snuggled down into the car seat and gave a contented little sigh of pleasure at being in the same car with him.

The pizza parlor was not yet crowded when we arrived, and usually I feel a little conspicuous walking into an empty room like that, but with Steve beside me I didn't mind feeling conspicuous. Just walking into the pizza parlor with him was probably raising my status at Wessconnett High by five points. I was so awed to be in his royal company that I even forgot to overrule Corky when he ordered anchovies on the pizza.

"How did it go last week in Raleigh?" Corky asked Rachel when the waitress brought us a pitcher of lemonade.

"Terrible," she said, her husky voice rich with tragedy. "Jill threw a shoe."

Steve looked startled. He seemed to think this was some sordid revelation about Rachel's home life.

"Jill is a horse," I explained.

He looked relieved.

"I guess you ride, too," he said to me.

Corky shot me an amused look.

"Actually," I said, "I'm kind of afraid of horses."

Rachel averted her head at this shameful confession, but Steve actually began to look more cheerful. I guessed it was a relief to him to know that he didn't have to admire

me. Even a hero-worshipping type must get
fed up now and then with admiring people.

"I don't like to have them stomping and
snorting right in my face," I explained.

"Aw, you don't really mind them," said
Corky. Corky was always unwilling to face
the truth about my basic cowardice.

"Not if they're small, quiet, and very,
very old," I agreed, trying to imagine a
horse the size and disposition of an aged
Saint Bernard.

"It's hard to believe you and Corky are
cousins," Steve remarked. "You seem
so...different."

"You think so?" I said. Actually, I
thought Corky and I were alike in lots of
ways.

"Gosh, yes," Steve said. "As different as
night and day. How did you say you two
were related?"

"Corky's mom and my mom are sisters," I explained. There was a kind of
pleasant symmetry in our family, I realized.
Mom had one sister, Aunt Myra, and Dad
had one brother, crazy Uncle Mark. The
symmetry broke down a little in my gener-
ation. Corky and I should have each had a
brother or sister, instead of us being only
children. Or else Uncle Mark should have
had a kid, at least, so I could have had a

cousin from Dad's side of the family as well as from Mom's. On second thought, however, I decided it was better to forget about symmetry. If Uncle Mark had a kid, I was sure it would be a horrible twerp.

"They're sure taking their time with that pizza," Corky said gloomily.

I knew I should have been glad the pizza was slow in coming. I needed to be making use of every one of these golden moments to make a good impression on Steve. But the trouble was, I was starting to be afraid to say anything for fear it would turn out to be wrong. Corky and Rachel immersed themselves in a technical discussion about an orthopedic-type shoe that would compensate for the damage Jill had done to her hoof at the Raleigh show, but I just sat in dumb silence, now and then managing a sickly smile at Steve. Steve didn't say much either. He seemed content just to gaze at me starry-eyed. When the waitress showed up with the pizza I took a slice of it and starting eating it with intense concentration, trying to avoid the anchovies.

"You know something, Fran?" Steve said. "I think you're a little bit shy."

At that Corky nearly choked on his pizza, and a wave of surprise spread across even Rachel's impassive countenance.

"That's okay," Steve went on dreamily. "I like shy girls."

After that, I really couldn't think of anything to say. I mean, I was positively afraid to say anything for fear of dispelling the illusion.

Steve opened the door for me as we filed out of the pizza parlor. "Maybe we can get together again soon," he said, smiling down at me.

I could tell he was trying to be extra nice because I was supposedly so shy, so I managed a weak smile.

"Could you just drop me off at my house?" I said to Corky as I got into the car.

"You aren't going back to the show?" said Steve.

"My folks are expecting me back early," I said. Actually, what was really going on was that trying to impress Steve was wearing me down. If he liked shy, I thought I could manage to act shy, but it was going to be hard work. And I wasn't sure how long I could keep it up. I was afraid if I got any more tired, I might pop out with some smart crack that would completely demolish his idea of me.

As soon as I got home, I fixed myself a glass of instant lemonade and collapsed on the couch. Mom found me stretched out there when she came in a little later with the groceries. "So how was your outing?" she said, setting the milk down on a footstool.

"I think Steve likes me," I said.

"That's good."

"But he doesn't know what I'm like," I said. "He thinks I'm sweet and shy."

Mom thought about it. "Well, you're sweet, anyway," she said.

Naturally, your mother thinks you're sweet, I thought. You'd be in pretty bad shape if your own mother didn't think you were sweet. I forced myself to get up from the couch. "You go lie down," I said, "I'll get the groceries."

She grinned. "I'm okay," she said. "I'm not the one that had the exhausting date."

"I guess I was trying too hard to impress him." I groaned.

When I got the first bag of groceries to the kitchen, Mom was putting soup on.

"Is Dad still over at the plant?" I asked.

"Yup. He wants to get everything in good shape for when the Chicago people show up on Monday. He called and said not to hold dinner for him."

"Mom, how long do you think it takes before you really feel comfortable with a new boy? I mean, a boy you're interested in dating."

"Depends," she said, stirring the soup. "With your Dad and me it didn't take long, but not everybody is as easy and old shoe as he is. People are different."

"I really think Steve likes me," I said.

"Why wouldn't he like you?" said Mom. "Better bring in the bag with the ice cream next," Mom said. "It's hot out there."

I went to get the bag with the ice cream. It was already dripping sticky drops as I brought it in. "He acted as if he were going to call," I said. "He said, 'Maybe we can get together soon.' Doesn't that sound as if he's going to call?"

"Sometimes they do and sometimes they don't," Mom said, tasting the soup.

That was not what I wanted to hear. I shoved the ice cream into the freezer, cold air streaming around me in white billows, then slammed the freezer door shut. "I think he'll call," I said. But I had an uncertain feeling. I wondered if I should have gone back to the horse show and worked some more on impressing him.

Chapter Three

The following week was the last week of school. Everybody was talking about what they were going to do during the summer. Claudia Martin had gotten a job at a summer camp.

"This year I'll only be a junior counselor," she explained to me, "but later on I can advance to senior counselor."

"What camp are you going to?" I asked.

"Camp Winnehutchee."

I remembered that was the one with the great-looking kitchen staff.

"But the important thing," Claudia went on, "is that I'll get a lot of good experience working with children. That will be really helpful to me later in my chosen profession of teaching.''

Somehow I had the feeling the kitchen staff was going to be wasted on Claudia.

"What are you doing this summer?" she asked.

"I'll be working around my aunt's farm," I said. "I'll do all her yard work and keep the vegetable garden. It's a big job, actually." I could hear myself sounding a little defensive.

It was Wednesday and still no call from Steve. I was beginning to wonder, as Uncle Mark would say, if I had backed the right horse.

"That sounds like quite a challenge," said Claudia. "Who knows? Perhaps your interest in horticulture will lead to a challenging and rewarding career." She looked as if she could go on in this vein for hours. "We should devote our high school years," she said, pink with enthusiasm, "to developing our full potential. Only real dedication and hard work can help us reach our final goals."

Claudia had a way of sounding like a speech at graduation. It was amazing how quickly her conversation caused the old eyes to glaze over with boredom.

By Wednesday evening I was beginning to have serious misgivings about my decision to spend the summer in Wessconnett. Of course, in my heart I knew I wouldn't have been as good a camp counselor as Claudia. Her small talk might be deadly, but she was Nash County's female fencing champion and had often bored me with accounts of her feats at rappelling and white water canoeing. No doubt there was a lot the little campers could learn from Claudia. Which is more than you could say for me, I thought gloomily. Every day that passed without Steve's calling me up made me feel that much more inadequate.

At eight o'clock the phone rang. I raced to it. "Hello," I said breathlessly.

"Hi, Fran. It's your Uncle Mark."

"Oh...hi, Uncle Mark."

"Is anything wrong?"

"No, nothing's wrong. I was just expecting a call from somebody else," I said. "You want to talk to Dad?"

"In a minute. Right now I want to talk to you. Junco and I have got a new apartment right on Central Park, and we were wondering if you'd like to come up for a week or so and see New York."

"I don't think so, Uncle Mark. This isn't a very good time."

"What do you mean?" he boomed. "It would be a terrific experience, a magnificent experience for you. I could devote my whole week to showing you around, give you the insider's view of the city. You don't want to spend your entire life in that little one-horse town, do you?"

"The thing is," I said, "I've got a summer job helping Aunt Myra with the yard and the garden. I can't let her down."

He brushed that aside. "Myra would let you off the hook," he said. "This would be an educational experience. I've already got tickets to *Moonshine Magic*, and believe you me, I had to pull some strings to get those. The scalpers are getting $200 per, when they can get them. Fran, I tell you, you're going to love it."

"I'm going to be sorry to miss it," I said firmly. "Let me get Dad." It was so typical of Uncle Mark to have gotten tickets for a show I didn't want to see when I hadn't even agreed to come.

"I'll bet you're interested in some boy down there," he said suspiciously. "That's it, isn't it?"

"Dad!" I called. "It's for you. It's Uncle Mark."

"Dammit, Fran, listen to me when I'm talking," Uncle Mark said.

"Excuse me, Uncle Mark. What were you saying? I was just trying to get Dad."

"Now listen, Frances. Take the advice of an older and wiser man, and don't go getting serious about some boy at your age."

"I'm not serious about any boy, Uncle Mark. I think Dad must be out front. Just a minute and I'll go get him."

I laid the phone down on the counter.

Actually, Uncle Mark could be pretty funny when he started lecturing, but right then I wasn't in the mood to snicker at his sermons. I was too discouraged about my love life to have the strength to snicker at anything.

I found Dad out front getting set to change the oil in the car. He always tried to change his own oil. Dad and Mom were the type of people who washed tinfoil and reused it. A penny saved is a penny earned, they always said. My grandparents were like that, too. I didn't know how to explain Uncle Mark. He was not, to put it mildly, typical of the family. "It's Uncle Mark on the phone," I said.

Dad looked at the drop pan, the old rags, and the stack of oil cans he had assembled for the job. "Why can't he call on Sunday afternoon like everybody else?" he grumbled. But he went in.

As I got started putting the dishes in the dishwasher I could hear Dad in the family room telling Uncle Mark that as far as he knew I wasn't interested in any boy. "She's only fifteen, Mark," he said.

I could have told him that wasn't the line to take with Uncle Mark. Since he ran away from home at sixteen, he probably had a very distorted idea of the ages at which people could make messes of their lives.

By the time Dad finally got off the phone it was pitch black outside and too dark to see to change the oil, so he resignedly put all the junk up in the storage room again and came in the kitchen to get a cup of coffee.

"I think Uncle Mark has a nerve to quiz you about my personal life," I said hotly. "Who does he think he is?" I finished stacking the glasses on the top shelf and started gathering up the silverware.

"He's just taking an interest," said Dad. "Don't get so worked up about it."

"Taking an interest," I snorted. "He's probably the most interfering, bossy person I've ever known. I wish he'd have some kids of his own and quit bothering me."

Dad looked uncomfortable. He didn't like me to criticize Uncle Mark. I reminded myself that, after all, they were brothers. I supposed they were fond of each other. I already felt sorry that I had upset Dad, so I added quickly, "Of course, I guess he means well."

"That's right, kitten," said Dad. "He just wants you to be happy. He'd like for you to come up to New York and let him show you around. You might like to do that. Get to know him a little better."

"No, thanks," I said. "I'd just get dragged to play after play, then have to go backstage and be introduced to a bunch of strangers. You wouldn't want to do it yourself."

"Maybe not," he admitted. "But then I'm getting kind of set in my ways."

Just then the phone rang, but by then I was feeling so deeply and crushingly discouraged I didn't even go to answer it. Mom called from the family room, "Fran, it's for you."

I dropped the silverware into the sink with a big crash and ran into the family room.

"Hello?"

"Hi, Fran. It's Steve."

I melted into a chair, taking care not to lose my grip on the phone.

"Hi, Steve," I breathed. This was it. This was the moment I had been waiting for. If he had only called to ask me to buy a magazine subscription or sign a petition or something, I was just going to die.

"I was just wondering if you'd like to go to the movie Friday night," he said.

"I'd love to."

"Well, great! How about I pick you up at eight. Okay?"

When I waltzed back into the kitchen Mom and Dad looked at me curiously.

"Steve has asked me out," I said.

"Is this the fellow who thinks you're shy and sweet?" asked Mom.

"That's right," I said. Now that I was giddy with happiness, that little discrepancy between Steve's illusion about me and the reality didn't bother me a bit.

Dad picked up the evening paper. "Maybe she can break the truth to him gently," he said.

"That's what I'll do," I said. "I'll start out small by letting it out that I don't believe in the Tooth Fairy, then I'll gradually work up to telling him how Mrs. Mizell said I was a disruptive influence in Sunday school, and gradually he'll get to know the real, cynical, wisecracking me."

"Take it easy," Dad said, folding the paper back into the comics. "You don't want to shock the boy out of a year's growth."

It seemed like a long time until Friday, but at least all during those last two days of school I had the comfort of knowing that I was going out on a real date with Steve soon. And even nicer than knowing it myself...was being able to let Claudia know it.

"Just think," she said on Friday. "Tonight I'll be on my way to Camp Winnehutchee. I just feel in my heart that this is going to be a positive growth experience, that I am going to learn from those campers as well as teach them."

"That's wonderful, Claudia," I said. "All I'll be doing tonight is sitting in some dumb movie with Steve Blumenthal."

"Steve Blumenthal," she said weakly. I could see I had her on the ropes now. "I didn't know you two were dating," she said.

"But honest, Claudia," I said, "a positive growth experience like Camp Winnehutchee is much nicer than some dumb old date."

"It'll be cool in the mountains, too, not hot like here," she said feebly. But I could tell she would have happily traded all the summer's growth experiences for a date with Steve Blumenthal. All in all, it was a satisfying conversation. I had gotten tired of feeling inferior about all that white water rafting.

When Friday evening finally arrived, I had a lot of trouble deciding what to wear. Then all of a sudden I remembered a dress Uncle Mark had sent me. I had never worn it, and it was still packed in tissue paper in a box high up in my closet. Standing on a chair, I pulled the box down. When I spread the dress out on the bed, I knew right away that it was perfect. In sizes Uncle Mark knew to buy me a junior nine, but in styles he still leaned toward toddler two. I couldn't say the dress actually had dancing lambs and bunny rabbits on it, but it had been designed in that spirit, all right. It was a pale pink with some ruffles and lots of skirt. I slipped into it and was relieved to see that it fit perfectly. All it needed was pressing. It was a lucky break that I had remembered it, because I didn't have a single other dress that would so perfectly fit Steve's image of me as a sweet, shy girl.

When I went into the living room to check myself in the big mirror, Dad lowered his newspaper and looked at me appreciatively. "Now, that looks really adorable, kitten," he said.

"That's good...I guess," I said. It seemed like eons ago that I had been trying to look like a person with an interesting past.

Dad gave the newspaper an impatient shake and folded it back. "The SBI says they're closing in on a statewide drug smuggling ring," he said, "but I'll believe it when I see it. They never seem to catch that scum."

"Maybe they will this time," I said, looking over my shoulder to check my back hem in the mirror. "One of the SBI's people came to speak at assembly last month and she seemed to really know what she was doing." Wessconnett High was always bringing women with important jobs to speak to us. As I looked at myself in the mirror I remembered last month's speaker, Ms Margaret Simmons, investigator and crack crime buster for the State Bureau of Investigation, and was suddenly sure she wouldn't be caught dead dressed in pink ruffles. In all this pink and with my sweet-looking face, all I needed was wings and I could have passed for the Good Fairy. I think I have fairly conservative taste in clothes, but there was something about the sight of all the pale, baby-pink that made me want to rush right out and buy a belt with some spikes on it.

Steve was on time to pick me up. As we drove off, he patted me on the knee. "I've always wanted to get to know a sweet, old-fashioned girl,'' he said softly.

He was not making it any easier for me to let him get to know the real me.

When we got to the theater, he hopped out and opened the door for me. I concentrated on trying to float gracefully out of the car while in my mind I kept repeating the words ''sweet and shy'' over and over like a charm. I had this constant fear that if I let my concentration slip, some smart-alecky remark was going to escape my lips before I knew it.

Loads of kids I knew were milling around in the theater lobby. Brenda Spivey was behind us in the popcorn line. ''You and Steve make such a cute couple,'' she said, dimpling. It was just the sort of thing Brenda would say, I thought. Brenda really *was* sweet. No imagination, but sweet. I was a little shaken to see that even she was wearing cropped pants and barbaric-looking heavy jewelry. I was the only pink dress in the lobby. It was very possible, I thought uneasily, that I had overplayed my part a teensy bit.

Also I was beginning to have a kind of trapped feeling. Had I firmly sidestepped Uncle Mark's and Corky's schemes only to fall into a trap of my own making? I wasn't sure how long I could keep acting sweet and shy. I also wasn't sure I wanted to try to.

A minute later though we were settled into the plush theater seats clutching our hot popcorn boxes. Steve put his arm around me, which was nice. Looking at that gorgeous profile of his, lit by the flickering light of the screen, I found myself growing more philosophical. It wouldn't kill me to act shy for one summer, I decided. It certainly beat playing cards every evening with my parents. The only problem was I would probably have to buy some more disgusting pink dresses.

The movie turned out to be one of those things with lots of stars and no plot. You didn't have to get far into it to know that this was no *Gone with the Wind*. Steve seemed to like it well enough, though. As we filed out of the theater afterward he only had one complaint. "The people who made that movie didn't know much about planes," he said.

That just went to show how different people were. What spoiled the movie for me was that it had no plot, no characters, no directing, and no acting. But what spoiled it for Steve was that they had shown a DC-10 in a historical setting ten years before it was invented. "They ought to hire a technical advisor if they don't know anything about planes," he complained as he started up the car.

Since I was trying hard to be sweet I didn't point out that not one person in ten thousand gives a hoot when the DC-10 was invented. "You're right," I said meekly.

"There were some good things about it, though," he went on. "The way Anna sacrificed everything for her husband's sake, for instance. I liked that. It was inspiring, don't you think? I mean, that's what this country needs more of, self-sacrifice."

"Oh, you're right," I said. "You're absolutely right." The Anna character had struck me as pretty witless, but maybe I had been influenced by all I knew about her. She was played by Uncle Mark's second wife, Velma, who, as I knew, threw dishes when she got mad.

Actually, it was sort of scary how easy it was for me to fall into echoing Steve's opinions. I decided that possibly I had no personal integrity, a thought that did not cheer me up much.

When we got to my house, Steve walked me up to my front door. Then he bent over and kissed me on the forehead.

"I had a lovely time," I said insincerely.

He beamed at me. "Me, too," he said.

I went inside feeling depressed. Not only had I proved to myself that I had no personal integrity, I wasn't even having fun. Mom and Dad were playing Trivial Pursuit in the living room. They looked up as I came in. "Did you have a good time, dear?" Mom asked.

"It was okay," I said. "I'm still working on how to let him get to know the real me."

Mom turned her attention back to the game and plucked a card from the box. "Here's your literature question," she said. "Who said, 'Oh, what a tangled web we weave when first we practice to deceive'?"

"Uh, the Bible," said Dad. "No, wait. I take that back. Shakespeare."

"It was Scott!" crowed Mom. "I think I'm going to win this one."

I trudged upstairs gloomily. That Scott had a point, I thought. "A tangled web"— he had hit the old nail on the head that time, all right.

Very early the next morning I woke up with the feeling that I was starting off with a fresh, clean slate. I was not going to let the business with Steve get me down. It was a problem, but I would work it out somehow.

As soon as I grabbed a quick bite to eat I bicycled over to the farm. I wanted to get in some time on the garden before the day heated up. Corky was already out grooming Boss when I got there. As horses went, Boss was about as far as you could get from Devil. She was old and the satiny shine had long since left her coat, but she didn't seem to care. She looked slightly swaybacked and her lower lip sagged negligently, so you half expected to see a cigarette dangling from it. She looked like the sort of gambler that the hero should know better than to play cards with, the fellow that sits in the back of the saloon marking all the aces. But the truth was that Boss was worth her weight in gold to Rosemere Stables. Since she would never dream of kicking or biting or stomping or running away with anybody, the smallest child could be taught the basics of riding with perfect safety on her. I would have even been willing to get up on Boss myself except that I knew if I did, Corky would never give up until he had me on Devil.

Corky stopped brushing her as I leaned my bike against the stable. "How was the date with Steve?" he asked.

"Okay," I said.

"What do you mean, 'okay'?" he said darkly. "Look, Fran, if that guy gives you a hard time you let me know and I'll flatten him."

Actually, I was sure that if Steve ever gave me a hard time I could flatten him myself. He was rather willowy.

"It's not that," I said. "It's just that I'm not sure Steve is exactly my type." I added hastily, "Not that I'm ungrateful. I mean, he's very nice and all."

Corky went back to brushing Boss. "He is a bit of a dope, isn't he?"

I was a little annoyed. "If you knew that, why did you set me up with him?"

"I wasn't out to suit myself," said Corky. "I might have thought he was a dope, but you seemed to think he was the greatest thing since sliced bread."

"He is good-looking," I admitted. "Maybe I'll like him better after we've known each other awhile."

Corky just grinned.

"The only thing is," I said, "I just can't be myself around him. He seems to have this set idea about what I'm like, and I'm afraid anything I say will put him off. Did you ever have this problem with Rachel?"

He looked astonished. "Good grief, no." He reached for the hoof pick and started cleaning out Boss's hooves. She and Devil liked to stand in the muddy part of the north pasture and watch the cars go by on

State Road 43, so their hooves got pretty gunked up.

"Maybe I'm expecting too much," I said, wrinkling my nose. "After all, we've only gone out together once. Maybe everybody is a little stiff at first."

A small blue car turned off the highway and drove toward the stable. Corky cast it a glance. "That's Paige coming for her lesson," he said. "She always likes an early lesson."

The reason was no mystery to me. A seven A.M. lesson might leave you short of sleep, but it was the best way to catch Corky alone. By eight, the farm would be humming with workers, not to mention Uncle Joe and Aunt Myra.

Paige's face fell when she got out of the car and noticed me. I suppose as Corky was introducing us I should have set her mind at rest by explaining that we were cousins, not sweethearts, but for some reason I didn't want to. I guess it always annoyed me a little to see some girl gunning for Corky. I just nodded at her and moved over to the garden while they saddled up.

From the garden, where I was on my knees pulling weeds, I could hear Corky giving Paige her lesson in the small ring behind the stable.

"Sit back in the saddle," he was saying. "Sit well back. Slide that foot back. You've got a little too much foot there. Here, let me show you. Okay, now walk. Hands steady. Hold those hands in place just as if there were an imaginary horn there...cluck to her...get her to trot."

I had heard those instructions so many times I was sure I could have given the lessons myself.

"Turn your toes in to the horse...sit up!... Don't look down. Keep those shoulders square. Cluck to her. She's still walking. You've got to make her trot."

Anybody trying to make old Boss trot had my sympathy. It was all a person could do just to keep her awake. Apparently the frustration finally proved too much for Paige, because as I was rooting out a particularly stubborn weed, I heard her scream at Boss.

"Don't get mad at the horse," Corky said coldly. "She's putting up with a lot from you."

I could have told the girl that losing your temper with Corky's horses was not the way to his heart.

The wearying round of the lesson began again. "Remember to sit back in the saddle...turn those toes in...square those shoulders...pretend you have cups of coffee on your shoulders, keep them square, sit up straight.''

By the end of the hour, I had made a lot more progress with the weeds than Paige had made on Boss, which confirmed my suspicion that it was Corky she was interested in and not the horses.

After the lesson was over, Corky tied Boss at the side of the stable and Paige awkwardly dismounted. ''I think your balance is improving,'' said Corky, obviously looking for some crumbs of encouragement he could offer.

''Humph,'' said Paige. She shot a bitter glance in my direction. I was leaning back on my heels, resting from my labors. I smiled at her.

''I suppose your girlfriend over there rides, too,'' she said.

''Fran?'' Corky grinned. ''Oh, a first class horsewoman,'' he said.

As Paige slammed the door of her little car and sped off, I had the feeling she was crossing both horses and Corky off her list. Corky watched the car disappearing down the road. ''I'm afraid poor Paige is never going to learn to ride,'' he said.

It was already starting to warm up, and I decided to take a short break from my work. I perched on a barrel watching Corky groom Boss. A truck carrying farm workers turned in and moved back past the barn to the tobacco field.

"You don't like Steve much, do you?" I said.

"I like him okay," said Corky, hoisting the saddle off Boss and setting it on a fence railing. He checked her hooves, then picked up a brush. "I guess I feel sorry for him, that's all," he said, "with him coming so late in the year. I remember what it's like."

I peeled off my gardening gloves. "I can hardly remember when you moved here," I said. "It seems you've always been around."

"Well, I haven't," he said shortly.

In fact, Corky's family had only taken over his grandfather Hayden's farm when Corky was thirteen. Before that, Uncle Joe had managed a farm in Virginia. But Corky's family seemed so much at home, so nicely rooted now that it was hard to remember when they had moved back to Wessconnett, just as it was hard to remember that we had lived in Wisconsin when I was little. When I thought about it, I wondered if that was because things seemed to move so slowly in Wessconnett that it gave me the illusion that nothing had ever changed. There was just the quiet round of tobacco planting, tobacco harvest, pumpkin harvest, school opening, school closing, the steady parade of the seasons. Steve was the first new thing in my life in ages.

"You know, the thing about Steve," I said suddenly, "is that he kisses like a department store Santa."

Corky choked. I thought I heard him say, "Poor Steve," but he was spraying fly repellent so vigorously over Boss that the noise drowned him out.

"How does Rachel kiss?" I asked curiously.

"Look, Fran, that is a personal question."

"I'm sorry," I said.

Corky led Boss out from the rail. "Honest to Pete," he said, "if Steve has convinced himself you're shy, he ought to have his head examined."

As Boss passed by me, she turned a yellowed eye in my direction and heaved a huge, horsey sigh. It occurred to me that she had a very low opinion of human nature.

Chapter Four

On Monday, the Chicago executives of Dad's company came and departed. The plant gave a collective sigh of relief, and on Tuesday morning Dad put the last few things in his suitcase, getting ready to go off to one of the company's technical study sessions in Atlanta.

"Promise me," Mom was saying, "that you'll take the bedspread off that hotel bed as soon as you get there. I'm sure they never wash those bedspreads. They must be full of germs. And don't go staying up really late and getting yourself overtired."

Dad winked at me. "The cheese processors of America aren't exactly a wild bunch," he said. "Don't worry so much, Dorothy."

"I guess it just makes me nervous when you go off without us," Mom said. "Now promise me that you'll sit near an exit on the plane. And when the stewardess starts giving all those safety instructions don't try to look bored and sophisticated. Pay close attention."

"For Pete's sake," Dad said, rearranging his socks to make room for his shaving kit. It was times like this that you saw what a patient man Dad was. A lesser person would have probably pitched the shaving kit at her.

"I know I'm being silly," she fretted.

Dad didn't disagree. "Why don't you call up your sister and have her come over for lunch," he said. "That'll give you something to think about. I promise I'll call you the minute I get there."

"Maybe you're right," said Mom. "Maybe I'll call Myra. I could make a nice quiche," she said, already brightening a little at the prospect. "Will you get back in time for lunch, Fran?"

"Not today," I said. "It always takes me all morning to mow the lawn. I think I'll just stay and have lunch with Corky."

Dad snapped his suitcase shut. "If you're ready," he said, "I can drop you off on my way to the airport."

I dashed back to my room and grabbed a change of clothes. When I mowed the lawn at the farm I got so hot I liked to shower and change before lunch.

"I wish you weren't taking the first hop in that tiny little commuter plane," Mom fretted. "I can't believe those little planes are really safe."

Dad made his way toward the door, me following him. "Just give Myra a call," he said. "You'll feel a lot better."

"I wish you wouldn't act so superior," said Mom in exasperation. "You wouldn't like it if I were going away without you, either."

I went on out to the car, since it always took Mom a few minutes to issue final words of warning and advice. I was glad to get a ride to Aunt Myra's place. All that bike riding out there was great for the figure, but mowing the lawn was going to be enough exercise for one day.

When Dad finally got in the car and we drove away, he observed, "Your mom's a bit of a worrier."

A few minutes later when we pulled up at the farm I could see three tractors moving in a cloud of dust out in the field by the wood. In the small ring near the stable Corky was already giving a lesson to the Ferguson twins, and Aunt Myra was working with someone else over in the big ring nearer the road. I hadn't gotten an early enough start, I decided, looking dubiously up at the sun.

I gave Dad a last peck on the cheek before he drove off. "Have fun," I said.

"Don't worry," said Dad. "I'm already looking forward to the workshop on mold control."

After he drove off, I walked over to the machinery barn to get the lawnmower. It looked old and puny next to all the monster farm equipment in the barn, but that was because it was not a piece of Uncle Joe's up-to-date, bank-financed equipment. But it was my very own personal lawnmower, which I had bought secondhand from Alphonso Williams when he decided he'd rather perish than mow another lawn.

I rolled the mower over to the lawn. Then, bracing my foot against the machine, I pulled stoutly on the starter cord. Since I had been clever enough to put in a fresh spark plug, it started after only my third try. The machine roared and shuddered. I took my ear stoppers out of my pocket and stuffed them in my ears to dull the noise, then slipped on my safety goggles, and tied a bandanna around my hair to protect it from the dust. I gave the mower a hard push to get it moving, then pushed it slowly over the big lawn. If if hadn't been for Aunt Myra's enormous lawn, I wouldn't have had a summer job at all, so I should have been grateful to that grass, but it was hard for me to develop any affection for it when I had to mow it.

After the first half hour of mowing, my fingers felt numb from the vibration of the mower and my legs were tired. I stopped for water, but it didn't seem to help much. After an hour of mowing, I began to sympathize with the state of mind in which Alphonso had sold me the mower. And at the end of an hour and a half my thought processes seemed to have stopped entirely. All that remained in my brain was a deep and passionate hatred of grass.

As I was mowing the tricky part around the oak tree with all those bumpy roots sticking up, I noticed that Aunt Myra was waving her arms at me over by the driveway, trying to get my attention. I walked over to her, took out my ear plugs and pushed up my safety goggles. She seemed struck by my appearance. ''Do you feel okay, Fran?'' she asked. ''Your face looks so pink.''

I wished she'd get on with what she had to say, so I could finish mowing the lawn before I collapsed. ''I'm fine,'' I gasped.

''Well, don't overdo it,'' she said. ''I just wanted to tell you that I've got to go do some shopping and then I'm having lunch with your mother, but tell Corky I'll definitely be back at three for Mrs. Robbins's lesson so not to worry about that.''

''Okay,'' I panted. ''I'll tell him. Have a good time.''

I staggered back to the oak tree, where the lawnmower was still roaring and shuddering, and managed somehow to finish the last bit of lawn before expiring completely.

Afterward, it was all I could do to totter upstairs on stiff legs and take a shower. I felt as if I had been run over by a steamroller.

When I came down, my hair damp from the shower and feeling all clean in fresh clothes, Corky was already pulling lunch out of the refrigerator. ''Dad said he won't be in for lunch,'' he said. He set a can of cola at my place and put a bowl of potato salad on the kitchen table. ''Hot dogs okay?'' he said.

''Fine,'' I said, sinking into a chair.

"You'll never guess what that Ben Ferguson did today," he said, dropping a few hot dogs into a pan of boiling water. "He stood right up in the saddle."

"He *what*?"

Corky laughed. "He's got a heck of a lot of confidence, that's for sure."

"I'm surprised he didn't kill himself," I said with a shudder.

"For a second, I admit, I was scared. I could see myself trying to explain to Mrs. Ferguson how I'd happened to let her darling boy break his neck. But he was on Devil, and Devil's awfully steady. If you keep your head, you can do just about anything on him."

I had heard Corky on this theme before, but I had never found it very convincing. I picked up a forkful of potato salad. One thing about mowing lawns, I thought. You can positively gorge yourself and not put on an ounce.

I was already recovering from my wiped-out feeling. Having lunch with Corky always perked me up. I couldn't put my finger on exactly why, but just having him in the same room made me feel better. His back was to me now as he put some hot dog buns on a cookie sheet, and I could see light glinting on the fine hairs of his neck where the thick dark curls of his head gave way to the fine blond ones of his neck and shoulders. Under his blue shirt you could sense the curve of his backbone and see the thickness of muscle straining against the shirt. He had a way of looking as if the seams of his shirt might give way any minute, especially around the shoulders. He could demolish the sleek look of the most expensive shirt in town. I supposed the final effect wasn't exactly elegant, but I liked it. A beautiful profile isn't everything, I thought, my mind turning in spite of myself back to Steve.

I had promised myself that I wasn't going to let my problem with Steve get to me, but I couldn't seem to stop thinking about it. My romance wasn't turning out to be quite as much fun as I had expected. There was no getting around it; acting sweet all the time was bound to be quite a strain. I could imagine if Steve kept asking me out, I might spend the whole summer doing nothing but agreeing with him and searching ever more desperately for additional ruffled dresses, which are not that easy to find these days.

And as long as I was just playing a part, I realized, there wasn't going to be any communication at all between Steve and me. Even if he were falling for me, it would be like the plot of that ballet where the guy falls in love with a mechanical doll. It wouldn't really be me he liked but my performance as a sweet, old-fashioned girl. Was I that desperate for a boy to go out with?

Since the answer to that question seemed to be yes, I tried to force myself to look at the whole thing in a more positive way. After all, I told myself, there is a little bit of a communication problem with everybody in the world. It's all a matter of degree. Everybody kept some of their thoughts bottled up inside. Even with Corky I didn't say everything that was on my mind. He was one of the people I liked best in all the world, but if I were to come right out and say something sweet to him like, "You light up my day," he would probably have dropped all the hot dogs on the floor, I thought, smiling a little at the idea.

"What's so funny?" he said, casting me a glance as he dumped the hot dogs onto a plate.

"I was thinking how lots of times you can't tell people about the way you feel," I said.

"Try me," he said.

"Well, like I was thinking just now about how much I care about you."

The plate of hot dogs slipped from his hands and shattered.

I looked down at the floor. "I don't think we'd better eat those," I said. "They might have splinters of glass in them or something."

Corky was down on his knees and began grimly picking up hot dogs and pottery shards.

"You see," I said. "That proves what I've been saying. I mean, you're like my own brother practically, but if I say anything sweet to you, you dump the hot dogs."

"I didn't dump the hot dogs. I just lost my grip on them for a second. I think the plate was wet. Slippery."

"Oh. I thought you were a little startled, maybe."

"Not a bit."

By the time Corky finished putting the hot dogs and the broken dish into the trash and had put a jar of peanut butter on the table, the color had returned to his face. "I guess you're thinking about your problem talking to Steve," he said, calmly enough.

I leaned my chin on my hands. "Right," I said. "I don't think Steve really wants to know what I'm like. Why else does he keep saying things like 'You're shy' and 'You're a sweet old-fashioned girl.' He keeps telling me what I'm like instead of asking me. Do you see what I mean? It's an interesting example of the failure of communication in the modern world."

Corky spread peanut butter on his bread deliberately. "You don't think it's just another example of how Steve is a dope?" he said.

"You may have a point there," I admitted, reaching for the knife and spreading some peanut butter on my own bread. "He is kind of heavy going. He's just so different from me it's like being out with somebody who lives on another planet. But I've got to persevere." I took a bite of the sandwich. "The fact is, I'm not getting any younger. It's time I had a romance."

"What's the sense of having a romance with somebody you don't even like?" said Corky.

"Well, there's the status, for one thing," I said thoughtfully. "I get points for going out with such a good-looking guy. You don't have to make a face at me, Corky. I'm just being honest. Then, the other thing is— it's an interesting experience. I've never had somebody open doors for me and act as if they were getting a crush on me."

Corky gave a disgusted little snort.

"You're somebody to preach," I said hotly. "Look at Rachel."

"That's different," he said. "I like Rachel okay."

"I've never heard you say anything good about her except that she could ride. Perhaps," I said airily, "there is smoldering passion in that relationship and you have been too discreet to tell me about it, but I don't believe it for a minute." I bit into my sandwich with decision.

When I looked up I was surprised to see that Corky was grinning at me. "Okay," he said, "have it your way. Have fun with Steve."

But that was precisely the trouble, I reflected glumly. I couldn't seem to have much fun with Steve. It was too bad that Steve wasn't more like Corky. I didn't have to get dressed up head to toe in pink and coo all evening to suit Corky. He and I understood each other.

Chapter Five

After lunch, I threw my old clothes into the back seat of the car and Corky drove me home. It's only a few miles from his family's place to our house. The fields and country roads quickly gave way to the tight little suburban streets at the edge of town where we live. Then when Corky turned the corner onto Oak Street I saw that the Rescue Squad's ambulance was stopped in front of my house. "Corky!" I cried. I couldn't say anything else. The men were just in the process of sliding a stretcher in. Aunt Myra scrambled into the ambulance behind the stretcher, then the doors were slammed shut. The ambulance's red light began to rotate slowly, and the siren started up with an uncertain moaning sound as the ambulance pulled away.

I felt frozen. When we reached the house, the ambulance was already ahead of us, turning and disappearing down Baker Street. "It's Mom," I said in an agony of apprehension. "I know it's Mom."

"Calm down," said Corky, following in the path of the ambulance as it sped ahead of us. "They take people to the hospital in ambulances all the time these days."

I didn't say anything. There was no use pretending that people called an ambulance to attend to the average hangnail. I knew this was an emergency.

The siren was now in full voice, and it was harder for us to keep the ambulance in sight as it sped up. We lost it finally at Third and Humber when it ran a red light.

"I don't think we'd better run the light," said Corky, pulling to a stop. "We might get ourselves killed."

He was right. The minute the ambulance had passed, the gap that cars had cleared for its passage closed up, and the east-west traffic started running again at full speed.

"We'll just go straight to the hospital," Corky said. "Which one first?"

"Community Hospital," I said quickly. "It's closest." Luckily, Wessconnett had only two hospitals, small, private Community Hospital, and big, public Wessconnett General.

The minute we pulled up to Community Hospital I knew we had chosen the wrong one. Sitting quietly among shade trees and broad lawns, it did not have the look of a place where an ambulance had just pulled up. Corky drove around back to the emergency entrance and, leaving me in the car, dashed into the building. I didn't bother to get out. I knew we were at the wrong place.

He ran out again and jumped in the car. "They didn't come here," he said. "They told me the Rescue Squad always takes people to Wessconnett General."

He did a quick U-turn and sped out of the parking lot toward the other end of town. It seemed like the longest drive of my life. Everything went wrong. First we got caught at a train crossing. Then just as we were pulling onto Grace Street, a policeman flagged us down to make way for a funeral procession.

As the long line of cars passed by with their lights on, I began to feel I couldn't stand it. I wanted to be moving toward the hospital so much that I could have gripped the bumpers in my teeth and dragged the car forward by myself. I noticed something else, too. When you are following an ambulance, being stopped by a funeral procession does not give you a feeling of optimism.

When we got to Wessconnett General, I threw open the car door and almost ran into the emergency room. The woman behind the cashier's window moved with the speed of a two-toed sloth. I gritted my teeth as her finger slowly followed the list of recent admissions. "Here we are," she said in the slow, measured syllables of one for whom time has lost its meaning. "Mrs. Dorothy Delacorte. She's been taken to the cardiac care unit, eighth floor." She then informed me that visitors had to enter through the lobby of the hospital instead of going directly up in the elevator by the emergency room.

With Corky following, I dashed out of the building again and went around the enormous, blank-looking hospital until at long last I found the front entrance. Glass doors gave onto an enormous, intimidating expanse of green carpeting. In the unearthly silence of the vast lobby, we made our way to the elevator. But when at last the elevator doors opened at the eighth floor, the unreal quality of the whole experience began to dissipate. Ahead of us, in a little waiting room at the turning of the corridor, I saw Corky's mom. She smiled and waved when she saw us. I let out a relieved sigh. Aunt Myra wouldn't be smiling and waving if things were really bad.

"Dorothy's resting comfortably," she said cheerfully as we rushed up. "We've had a scare, but the doctor thinks it's nothing serious."

"Where's Mom?" I asked.

Aunt Myra indicated an open door. "In there in the cardiac care unit," she said. "But she's asleep now."

"Can't I see her?"

I guess Aunt Myra could see how I felt because she didn't try to reason with me; she just took my hand and led me over to the door of the room. There were several beds in there and it took me a second to see Mom; then things seemed to go foggy for a second or two as I saw all the dials and lights attached to her bed.

"You better sit down," said Corky in a worried tone.

I could see he was right and tottered back to the orange plastic couch where Aunt Myra had been sitting. There were heaps of crossword puzzles stacked on the table near it. The hospital seemed to have decided that

doing crossword puzzles was the perfect oc-
cupation for the families of heart attack
victims.

"We had just finished the quiche Dorothy had made," Aunt Myra was saying,
"when I noticed she wasn't looking too
well. She said she had a pain in her chest, so
I called the Rescue Squad." She sat down
and stretched out her legs. "Of course, now
they have all those monitoring devices
hooked up to her, and if anything goes
wrong there'll be doctors running in there
right away, but Doctor Frankel says if it was
a heart attack, it must have been a very mild
one and he doesn't think there's any cause
for alarm. We'll know more after we get the
results from the blood tests."

None of that sounded so bad. I couldn't
figure out why I felt so weak. Corky
slumped down in a chair and stretched his
long legs out in front of him. It was funny,
I thought with odd detachment, how alike
family members could be at times. Corky
and Aunt Myra both had that way of kicking their legs out in front of them. I felt as
if I were watching the scene from a long way
off—Corky and Aunt Myra and the cold
cigarette stubs in the ashtray and the piles of
crossword puzzle books.

"Fran and I have had a rotten half hour," Corky said. "We had the devil of a time getting to the right hospital."

"Well, it's all okay now," said Aunt Myra. She looked at me critically. "Corky, maybe you'd better take Fran home and let her rest. She looks pretty shaken up."

"No, I'll stay here with you," I said. "I want to be here when Mom wakes up."

"You're only going to upset her if you look as if you're about to faint," Aunt Myra said. "Besides, I think you'd better try to get in touch with your father. Even though it doesn't look serious, I know he's going to want to know that Dorothy is in the hospital."

I suddenly sat up straight. "Oh, my gosh, yes," I said. "I'd better try to call him right away."

"Corky will take you back home," said Aunt Myra, "so you can look for the phone number of his hotel. I'll call you if we need you here, but I think the thing for you to do after you call your dad is just to get some rest. Everything's under control."

Corky practically had to lead me back to the car. I felt very strange. "Are you okay, Fran?" he asked.

"I guess I'm still feeling a little bit shaky," I said.

"It looks like everything's okay."

"My mind knows that," I said. "It's just that my knees haven't realized it yet. Tell me the truth, Corky—do you really think it isn't serious?"

"Sure," he said. "But they have to play it safe and have it checked out."

I thought of all those dials and tubes at Mom's bed and felt chilled. "I could never be a doctor or anything like that," I said. "I'm too much of a coward."

"Don't start that," said Corky irritably. "You aren't a coward."

I stifled a little smile. It was nice to be back having the same old argument with Corky. I was feeling better already.

Corky wanted to hang around the house a little to make sure I didn't pass out or anything. For somebody who kept insisting I wasn't a coward, he seemed to be pretty uneasy about me falling apart. "Go on home," I insisted. "I'll be okay. Besides, if you don't go, who's going to be there when Mrs. Robbins comes for her lesson?" I finally pushed him out.

Then I began the search for Dad's number. The first place I checked was the refrigerator door, which is where we put grocery lists, but there was no number posted there. Then I looked on the bulletin board, which is where we pin memos like the month's school lunch menus. It took me a little longer to eliminate the possibility the number was there, because the bulletin board was so studded with layers upon layers of paper that it looked as if a metropolitan phone book had had a nervous collapse all over it. When I tried to peer underneath one of the top layers of paper, the pins holding them slipped out, and papers slid down and all over the kitchen floor. I finally had to take everything off the bulletin board and go through all the scraps of paper one by one. There was no sign of Dad's phone number anywhere.

I couldn't believe that Mom had let Dad leave town without getting the hotel or the number where he could be reached. She was too much of a worrier for that. It had to be around somewhere.

I checked the phone book cover for penciled notes. Finally, as a last resort I went into Mom and Dad's room to look in Mom's desk. It had always been a rule of the house that nobody was to go into Mom's desk. I think this was partly because it was such a pretty, delicate old desk, one that had belonged to her grandmother, and partly because when I was little she was afraid I would bother the important papers she kept there. She had always kept it locked, but I found the key in her jewelry box and unlocked it. Unlocking it felt weird. I had never opened the desk before. Now that I was older, I supposed there was no particular reason for that anymore, but it still felt strange to be opening the fancy inlaid cover and folding it down.

When it was folded down, the inlaid cover of the desk turned into a writing surface and a double row of small pigeonholes was revealed. That was where Mom had stuffed receipts to be saved for income tax time. Then below the pigeonholes was a row of tiny drawers for things like stamps and paper clips and below the drawers, on the back surface of the desk itself, Mom had put stacks of papers. All at once I saw a square of paper lying just in front of those stacks of papers. It had the penciled notation "Holiday Motor Inn" and a phone number. I sighed with relief, but as I picked up the square of paper and lifted the inlaid cover to close the desk up again, I noticed something odd. Underneath one of the bulky stacks of papers on the desk was a black photograph album almost completely hidden by the papers.

That's strange, I thought. I knew that our photo albums weren't black. They had bright leatherette covers. It seemed peculiar to find this album I'd never seen tucked away with all the family business papers. But I had more important things to do than poking around among the papers, so I closed the desk and went to call Dad. As it turned out, he had not yet gotten to his hotel, but the person at the desk promised to give him my message as soon as he arrived.

I went into the living room and threw myself down on the couch. The house was so eerily empty, I began to wish I had asked Corky to stay on with me after all. Finally, I jumped up and phoned the hospital. They put me through to the waiting room on the eighth floor.

"Aunt Myra?" I said. "How is Mom doing?"

"Fine," she said. "Still asleep. They gave her a sedative, you know. Dr. Frankel was just by to check on her and he said she really looks good. There's positively no reason to worry at this point. Is Corky there with you?"

"No. I made him go home. He had to give Mrs. Robbins a lesson at three."

"I wish he had stayed with you," said Aunt Myra. "I don't like you to be alone there letting your imagination run away with you. When is your father going to get home?''

"I haven't been able to get through to him yet. His hotel is supposed to give him the message when he comes in.''

"Go watch television or something. You sound edgy to me. Just remember your mom's getting the very best of care. There's no problem here whatever.''

After I hung up, I realized Aunt Myra was right. I was edgy. I wished Corky were with me. But it couldn't be long, I told myself, until Dad got my message. Then he would call. How I longed to hear the sound of his voice! I knew I'd feel a lot better after I talked to him.

I threw myself down on the couch, closed my eyes, and tried to make my mind a blank. The longer I did that, oddly enough, the more the black photo album insisted on floating up in it.

Finally I got up from the couch. It was clear I needed something to think about, something to take my mind off my troubles. Maybe I would just go and find out what was in that black photo album.

Chapter Six

I lifted the pile of bulky papers up and carefully slid the photo album out from under them. I straightened the papers up again afterward. I could imagine what Mom would say if I messed up all her carefully arranged papers. Then I sat down on the bed and opened the album.

I saw right away it was fairly old. For one thing, the first page was pictures of Uncle Mark, and they had been taken while he still had all his hair. Also, I would judge they were taken while he was a starving young actor because he sure looked like he could have stood a square meal. One of them showed him leaning against the side of a bridge. A girl was with him and behind them were some old buildings with a big, pointy-topped clock. I thought it looked like Big Ben in London. It was funny to be looking at pictures of Uncle Mark taken when he was probably not much older than I was now and to realize he was alone in a foreign country and apparently already having a romance. The girl looked ridiculously sweet and insipid but I didn't hold that against her. I had the same problem myself and look at how sharp a mind I turned out to have when you got to know me.

I turned over to the second page and was astonished to see it was a bunch of wedding pictures. So Uncle Mark married Sweetsie Face. But then why not? He had married all kinds of people. I guess he just never got around to mentioning this one.

I leafed casually over to the next page and was suddenly caught up short. Uncle Mark and Sweetsie Face had a baby? I didn't see how anybody could forget to mention they had a baby. Maybe something awful had happened to it and Uncle Mark didn't like to mention it. Quite possibly they had forgotten to feed it or something basic like that. He and Sweetsie Face only looked like kids themselves.

There were a couple of snapshots of the mother with the baby, the flashbulb making everybody's faces look like blobs of dough swimming in darkness. But on the next couple of pages I saw that the proud parents had obviously taken advantage of a package photo offer because it was a set of professional portraits of the baby, who, now that I got a good look at it, looked oddly familiar.

I glanced at the photo of me as a baby that was on Mom's dresser and realized that Uncle Mark's baby looked like me. That was why it seemed familiar. Family resemblances were certainly odd things. Uncle Mark's baby and I could have been sisters. In fact, we were even wearing the same little pink checked dress. A hand-me-down? I thought. A wild coincidence? But suddenly a chill went down my back. I saw that there was a hole in the black paper where one of the photos had been torn out, leaving half of the page with a blank place, and I found my eyes drawn sharply back to the photo on Mom's dresser.

Without really thinking the thing through, I found myself pushing a chair up against the tall dresser, standing on it, and

taking the photo down. I struggled to slide
the felt backing out of the frame until I finally unwedged it and slid the photograph
out from between its frame and the backing. As I had feared, there was a bit of torn
black paper stuck to the back of the photo.
It was roughly in the shape of a boot. It
should be pretty easy, I realized, to check
and see if this torn piece of black paper
matched the missing piece in the photograph album, but I seemed to have a hard
time making my feet walk back to the bed
where the album was lying open.

When at last I approached the album I
could see at once that the missing piece of
paper was boot-shaped. I laid the photo
back in the album and it fit perfectly. There
has to be some logical explanation for all
this, I thought, sitting on the bed in a daze.
There has to be some perfectly simple reason why Mom has had a picture of Uncle
Mark's baby on her dresser for fifteen years
and has acted as if it were me.

With a sort of cold feeling in my stomach
I went over to the desk and took out the
stacks of bulky papers. I was past caring
whether Mom would be upset about things
being disarranged. I slowly and methodi-
cally began going through every one of the
papers. I wasn't exactly sure what I was

looking for, but all the family's important papers were in Mom's desk, so if there was any information around about that photo, I thought it must be there.

In the stack there were fancy-edged stiff pieces of paper that seemed to be from banks, a handful of old savings passbooks, the deed to the house, and what seemed to be endless insurance policies. I was almost at the bottom of the stack that had covered up the album when I found a copy of a birth certificate. Naturally it caught my eye at once because it had my name on it—Frances Louise Delacorte. The only problem was it didn't have Mom's and Dad's names on it. In fact, at first glance it looked like the birth certificate for a person who had never existed. I had never heard of her, anyway. She had been born in Sheffield, England, and was the daughter of Mark Antony and Frances Wostenholm Delacorte.

There has to be some explanation for this, I thought desperately. And if Mom weren't flat on her back in a hospital bed I would ask her for it. I was probably not thinking too clearly because of the rough day I'd had, but somehow I felt afraid. Corky. I would go find Corky.

I carefully put everything back as nearly as possible to the way I had found it. I even managed to get the baby photograph back in its frame and back up on Mom's dresser. I looked around the room before I left. Everything looked cool and neat. To look at it now you would never guess anything had happened.

I fled the house and bicycled full speed all the way out to Corky's house. It was a wonderful relief to be pedaling as hard as I could with the wind blowing my hair. The harder my legs went, the cooler my mind felt. I began to feel sure that there was a simple explanation for the whole thing.

When I pulled the bike up to the stable, I was out of breath. Through the door I could see Corky polishing a bridle spread over his knees. Behind him bales of hay were stacked to the ceiling. The barn cat was scaling the pyramid of hay, an eye out for mice. One of the horses stuck his nose out of his stall and snorted. I had seen the scene countless times before. It seemed impossible that it could be so unchanged if my life were really falling apart around me.

Corky heard me come in and looked up sharply. "Is everything okay?" he said. There was a smell of leather polish and brass polish in the still air, and the brass fittings on the leather straps glinted, making bright points of light in the dim, dusty stable. I didn't speak but leaned against the stable door, trying to catch my breath. Corky looked at me with alarm, then jumped up to get me some water. An old refrigerator was kept in the corner of the stable which always held, in addition to the various veterinary prescriptions for the horses, ice water. "Why didn't you call me?" he said. "I could have come to get you. What's wrong?"

I sat down on a bale of hay and choked down some water. "Mom's okay," I managed to say. "At least, I guess she is." I hesitated. This whole thing was so strange, I could hardly figure out how to begin. I gulped for air. "But the weirdest thing has happened," I said. "I mean, it's just so strange. You see, I had to go in Mom's desk to get Dad's phone number and I found...a birth certificate with my name on it."

Suddenly I knew I didn't have to go on. The look on Corky's face told me that he already knew all about it.

There was a long silence while I held my breath. "You knew," I said. I was surprised that the words came out in a whisper. I seemed to be losing my voice. I took a deep breath and this time speaking carefully I said, "You knew all the time that I was adopted." I felt as if I were choking.

"Why didn't you tell me?" I hated myself for it, but tears started streaming down my face.

Corky absentmindedly picked up the bridle he'd been polishing. "I wanted to tell you lots of times," he said. "But I thought it would get you upset."

"Oh, no," I said. "I'm absolutely tickled pink to find out that everybody I know has been lying to me all my life. I feel like a positively new person."

I felt a little stab in the heart when I said that because it was no joke. I really was a new person. I wasn't who I had thought I was at all. I had a strange sort of floating, disconnected feeling, as if I were a little piece of land that had come loose from the continent and was slowly drifting away.

"I may not even be an American," I said in alarm, suddenly remembering the birth certificate.

"Sure you are," said Corky. "Your father was an American, so that makes you one."

My father. He meant Uncle Mark. I had a definite sick feeling at the idea of Uncle Mark being my father. Why, I didn't even *like* him. I refused to think of Uncle Mark as my father, no matter what the birth certificate said. That much was settled.

First
Class
Romance

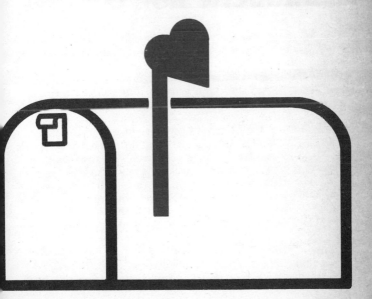

Delivered to your door by

First Love from Silhouette®

(See inside for special 4 FREE book offer)

Find romance at your door with 4 FREE First Love from Silhouette novels!

Falling in love for the very first time...what's it *really* like? It's easy to find out just how many ways love's magic comes to a girl like you, when you have First Love from Silhouette novels sent right to your home.

This is a special series written just for you, as you discover how warm, how special and how radiant romance can be. You can even receive these tender stories each month to read at home. All you have to do is fill out and mail back the attached postage-paid order card, and you'll get 4 new First Love from Silhouette novels absolutely FREE! It's a $7.80 value...plus we'll send you a FREE Mystery Gift. And there's another bonus: our monthly First Love from Silhouette Newsletter, free with your subscription.

After you receive your free books, you'll have the chance to preview 4 more First Love from Silhouette novels for 15 days. If you decide to keep them, you'll pay just $7.80— with no extra charge for home delivery and at no risk! You'll also have the option of cancelling at any time. Just drop us a note. Your first 4 books and the Mystery Gift are yours to keep in any case.

First Love from Silhouette®

A FREE Mystery Gift awaits you, too!

Mail this card today for your
4 FREE BOOKS
(a $7.80 value) and
a Mystery Gift FREE!

First Love from Silhouette®

Silhouette Books, 120 Brighton Rd., P.O. Box 5084, Clifton, NJ 07015-9956

☐ Yes, please send 4 new First Love from Silhouette novels and Mystery Gift to my home FREE and without obligation. Unless you hear from me after I receive my 4 FREE books, please send me 4 new First Love from Silhouette novels for a free 15-day examination each month as soon as they are published. I understand that you will bill me a total of just **$7.80** with no additional charges of any kind. There is no minimum number of books that I must buy, and I can cancel at any time. No matter what I decide, the first 4 books and the Mystery Gift are mine to keep.

NAME _____
                    (please print)

ADDRESS _____

CITY _____ STATE _____ ZIP _____

Terms and prices subject to change.
Your enrollment is subject to acceptance by Silhouette Books.

CCF565

"You aren't even my cousin," I said. My voice was definitely getting louder, but I was still thinking clearly. If Mom wasn't my mother, then it followed that Aunt Myra wasn't my aunt and Corky couldn't be my cousin.

Corky looked unhappy. "I think Dad's got some brandy in the house," he said. "Let me get it. It would be medicinal, kind of. You know, for when people have had a bad shock?"

"This is not a movie, Corky," I said in dire tones. "This is my life." I ran my fingers through my hair in a distracted way. I had just realized that I kind of looked like old Sweetsie Face in the photographs. It wasn't my mom's blond hair that I had at all, but the blond hair of Frances Wostenholm Delacorte, whoever she was. "I wonder what happened to Uncle Mark's wife," I said. I couldn't bring myself to call Sweetsie Face my mother. "Probably drank herself to death or something," I said gloomily.

"Do you have to take this so hard?" Corky said. "Lots of people are adopted. It's not the end of the world."

"I can't believe you would say such a stupid thing," I said.

Corky fell silent. I turned on my heel and headed out the stable door. He followed me. "I'll drive you home," he said.

"No, thank you," I said, reaching for my bicycle.

Corky grabbed my shoulder. "I'm driving you home," he repeated. "You're not going to go by yourself."

I had a momentary impulse to kick him, but he could so easily pick me up and carry me to the car and was so clearly determined to do it if necessary, that I decided to save myself the effort. I got into his car without saying a word.

As we were driving down State Road 43, I said dully, "I wonder what they were going to do when I got my driver's license. I would have had to show my birth certificate then. It was so dumb not to tell me. Everybody knows you're supposed to tell people they're...adopted." My voice still stuck at the word.

"Maybe it was your Uncle Mark's idea not to tell you," he said.

I groaned softly. I preferred not to think about Uncle Mark. I would rather concentrate on the treachery of my nearest and dearest like Mom, Dad, and Corky. That made me feel good and mad, which definitely was a better feeling than the sick feeling I got thinking about Uncle Mark and Sweetsie Face. "Maybe old Sweetsie Face abandoned me," I said. "Uncle Mark always did pick the most awful women."

"Sweetsie Face?" he said, looking puzzled. "Oh, you mean your mother."

I shuddered at the word. "Maybe I'll just be a citizen of the world," I said, "and not be anybody's kid at all. Who needs them?"

I felt as if I had come unplugged from everything that held me steadily in place. Even Corky looked different to me. I seemed to see him in brighter colors and he looked bigger and more fierce, somehow. My mind was whirling in a spiral. Uncle Mark was actually my dad, Dad was really my uncle, and Corky was no more related to me than anybody I might meet on the street, no more related to me than...Mom. Tears started streaming down my face again.

"For Pete's sake, Fran," said Corky helplessly, "I wish you wouldn't cry. I just hate it."

"I have a right to cry." I sniffled. "Nobody in Wessconnett has a better reason to cry right now than me. Why should you care?"

"It just makes me want to cry, too," he said glumly.

A little hysterical giggle escaped me, but the tears kept flowing down my cheeks. When we drove up into the driveway, I tried to wipe the tears off my face before I got out. I didn't want the neighbors to see me crying. Corky opened his door. "I'm going to stay with you until your dad gets home," he said.

"You are absolutely not," I said. I might be falling apart, but I could still draw a firm line. "You are not even *related* to me."

Corky looked stung. He didn't argue, though. He just walked me up to the door and stood there while I unlocked it.

"Well, we're still friends, aren't we?" he said.

I began to close the door. "I'll think it over," I said, "and let you know."

Corky put his foot in the door. "Look, Fran, am I supposed to keep this a secret from my mom and dad? Are you going to tell your dad that you know?"

"I haven't decided what I'm going to do yet," I said, "so keep it a secret. That shouldn't be hard. You're so good at keeping secrets."

He winced and I finally managed to close the door. I was already feeling bad about being nasty. Now that I was all alone in the world, I thought mournfully, I was going to need a friend more than ever.

I hadn't been back at the house long before the phone rang. It was Dad returning my call.

"Fran? Is everything okay?"

"More or less," I said, choking. I was doing my best to sound calm. "It looks as if Mom's had a heart attack, but not a very bad one at all. Anyway, she's in the hospital, and Aunt Myra thought you would want to know." All at once my voice sort of wavered and I started sobbing.

"Fran?"

"It's okay," I said, sniffling hard. "I mean, Mom's okay. But it's just been so scary. It's been such an awful day." Then I broke up and cried some more. I must have sounded really reassuring.

"I'm coming right home," he said, and he hung up.

I sat by the telephone for a while feeling sorry for myself and soon it rang again. It was Dad.

"Fran? I've called the airlines and the soonest I can get a flight is tomorrow morning. Maybe I should rent a car and drive?"

"No, Dad, really. It's okay. Why don't you call Aunt Myra? She's at the hospital still, I think, up on the eighth floor in the waiting room. She'll tell you Mom's doing okay."

"I'll do that," he said. "Now you just hang on, kitten. I'll be there as soon as I can."

After I hung up from talking to Dad, I went back into the bedroom, unlocked the desk and got the album out again. I kept looking into the faces of Uncle Mark and Sweetsie Face until my head ached. It was as if I thought by looking at the faces long enough, maybe I could understand the minds behind them. I looked then at my own face in Mom's dressing table mirror and compared it to Sweetsie Face's face. This was a little tricky to do because my eyes kept getting all blurry with tears. I didn't think we really looked that much alike, actually. But there was an over-delicate curve of the nose and mouth and a slight roundness of the cheek that gave us both that silly, sweet look. Frances W. Delacorte had a lot to answer for. Not only had she managed somehow to ditch me, but the only thing she had left me was that dumb face.

I finally closed the photo album and sat at Mom's dressing table for a while, holding my head in my hands. I had done so much crying that I had a headache. But I was slowly starting to see that when this piece of the puzzle of my life was fitted in, a lot of things made sense. I remembered, for example, the time Dad looked so uncomfortable when I said I wished Uncle Mark would have some kids of his own and leave me alone. Dad was probably thinking that Uncle Mark *did* have a kid of his own. I was it. At that thought I let out another groan.

Then there was Uncle Mark's nosiness. He probably acted that way because he still sort of felt as if he owned me. I realized now that part of the problem with Uncle Mark was that he didn't quite act like an ordinary uncle. He kept trying to get too close. He crowded me.

Now it occurred to me that if Uncle Mark found out I knew the truth he would crowd me even more. Once he no longer needed to pretend that he was only my uncle, I would be getting more and more invitations to come stay with him and Junco. He might even try to get me to come stay for good. How did I even know whether I was legally adopted? Maybe I was just sort of on loan to Mom and Dad.

Chapter Seven

Dad got in before lunchtime the next day. When I heard his key turn in the lock I ran to the front door and fell into his arms, weeping. "It's okay, kitten," he kept saying. "Mom's going to be fine."

It was awful to suddenly realize that Dad couldn't make my problems go away the way he used to when I was little. I supposed this was what it was going to be like to be grown-up. I didn't like it. To my surprise, he didn't even seem to realize that it wasn't just Mom's health that was worrying me.

"We'll go over together and see her," he said. "Then you'll feel a lot better. Myra says she's looking great. You didn't stay in the house by yourself last night, did you?''

"Aunt Myra did call and try to get me to come over to her place for the night, but I didn't want to go.''

"You should have gone with her, kitten. No wonder you're upset, sitting here all by yourself feeling low and lonely. I just wish I could have gotten home sooner.''

Dad couldn't know it, but my visions of Mom and Dad and Uncle Mark and Sweetsie Face were so bright and strong that last night it hadn't felt as if I were alone in the house at all. I had kept turning all those people over and over in my mind trying to make sense out of them. It hadn't been much fun, but I had figured it was better than going over to Corky's and trying to act as if everything were normal.

Dad went on into the bedroom to get together some things for Mom, like her toothbrush and nightgown. I didn't see how I could tell him and Mom what I had found out. What if the shock should give Mom another heart attack?

I realized that when I had complained about not being able to tell Steve what I was thinking, I hadn't known when I was well off. I hadn't known then what it was like to have a problem you couldn't talk to *any-*

body about. When I found out about my adoption, it was as if I had let an unfriendly genie out of a bottle. Already the genie had got one hand out and magically smashed my closeness to Corky. I was afraid if I didn't slam the lid back on, he might smash my relationship to my whole family.

"I'm just about ready to go," said Dad, coming into the living room. "I think I've got everything now. Or do you think she'll want bedroom slippers?"

Once he added the slippers to the little suitcase he had packed, we got in the car and drove toward the hospital. "You shouldn't let yourself get so upset," Dad said, giving me a comforting pat on the knee. "Everything's going to be fine. Now do your best to look cheerful when we get to Mom's room. We don't want to upset her."

When we got to Mom's room, she was sitting up in bed reading. They had moved her out of the cardiac care unit and into a regular room. Venetian blinds at the window divided the sun into neat bars that shone on the sheets of her bed, and on a table near her, carnations from the florist made a splash of red. It was great to see her sitting there looking like her old self again. She gave us each a big hug and immediately began moaning about the food they were giving her, so I knew she was back to normal. It became clear as she talked that she was not nearly so keen to have her bedroom slippers as she was to have a succulent steak and a chocolate eclair.

"I think they got my tray mixed up," she complained. "I got the salt free, sugar free, low fat, low cholesterol tray."

"What was on it?" Dad asked, with understandable curiosity.

"Just a napkin," said Mom bitterly. "Dr. Frankel wants to run some tests," she said. "Now that they've got me in here they don't want to let me go." She looked around the room critically. "Obviously, nobody would stay here unless somebody made them."

She brightened a little when Dad promised to come back after supper and play double solitaire with her.

"I think I'll skip coming this evening," I said. "This place gives me the creeps. I can't help it."

"You should go out with your friends and have a good time," Mom agreed. She heaved a sigh. "I wish I could be out tonight myself dining on pizza." She motioned to me to sit down on the bed, moving her legs over a bit to make room for me. I looked at her merry face, wreathed by crinkly blond hair, and found it hard to believe that she wasn't really my mother.

"Mom," I said, "how many times exactly has Uncle Mark been married?"

She made a helpless gesture. "It's so hard to keep track, isn't it?"

"I gave up years ago," Dad agreed.

"Well, when was the very first time he ever got married," I persisted. "You must remember that."

"Why this sudden morbid interest in your Uncle Mark?" asked Dad.

I didn't answer, but I was thinking that it was surprising, considering what a suspicious person I tended to be, that I had never realized something was wrong. Mom and Dad were very poor liars. It went against their nature to tell an outright lie, so they naturally shied away nervously when I approached the dangerous subject of my birth. If only I had known to watch, I would have probably seen lots of significant little signs. Now, for example, I couldn't ever remember Mom and Dad actually saying I had my mother's hair and my father's eyes. The most they had ever done was smile when other people had said it.

Of course, I knew what they would say if I confronted them with what I had just found out. They would say that they were my real parents because they were the ones who had brought me up, that there had been no deception at all. They would take the same line they had taken on Santa Claus. "Of course, there is a Santa Claus, Fran. He lives in all our hearts." That was the kind of approach I had to expect from them. I had long ago recognized that their notion of the truth wasn't quite the same as mine. Hadn't they told me that school would be fun, that shots didn't hurt much, and that I would never regret being honest? It was only what you expected from them— the cheerfulness line. But I hadn't expected Corky to give me a line. Corky and I looked at things the same way. Or that's what I had always thought.

"Don't look so down in the dumps," Mom said. "I don't think you are going to end up with a marriage a year the way your Uncle Mark has."

"Now, that's not quite fair, Dorothy," Dad protested.

"It's a slight exaggeration," said Mom, dimpling. "Now, you two—for dinner you can have the cold ham that's in the fridge. Fran can make a tossed salad. There's plenty of rice in the pantry, and I think those green beans in the crisper will still be good."

"We'll manage," said Dad. "Don't you worry about us."

I thought how typical it was of Mom to be thinking of food. If she'd gone into horses the way her sister had, instead of into quiches and chocolate cake, she might not be sitting in that hospital bed now. Well, at least, I thought glumly, I don't have to worry about her heart trouble being hereditary.

"Maybe you and Fran ought to take in a movie tonight or something," said Mom. "I can tell Fran needs some cheering up."

"I'm fine," I said, trying to look cheerful.

"Fran's fine," said Dad. "I'm going to come back here after supper and play cards with you."

After we left the hospital, Dad drove me home. We stopped off at a convenience store on the way to pick up a couple of TV dinners because neither Dad nor I had any intention of tossing salads and cooking green beans. Low as Mom's estimate of our cooking skills was, our real skills were even lower. Open and serve was about our limit.

Dad wanted to look in at the plant now that he was back in town, so after he took me home he drove off to work. He came in at six and helped me eat the TV dinners, then he went off to the hospital to visit Mom. I was alone again. I couldn't remember when I had so much time to think or so little that I really wanted to think about.

I realized that sooner or later I was going to have to face Corky. Aunt Myra didn't expect me to be over there puttering in the garden with Mom in the hospital, but eventually she would notice the grass was knee-high and the squash plants were overgrown with nut grass and would wonder what had become of me.

I wasn't sure why I was avoiding Corky. It wasn't just that I was angry with him, although I was very angry with him. The truth was that the solid ground of our relationship had shifted under my feet, and I felt as if I were losing my balance.

I lay down on the couch, my favorite brooding place, and stared at the ceiling, remembering how Corky had always squirmed whenever I teased him about our sharing the same cradle or about him being like a brother to me. If I thought anything about it all, I had thought he hated sentimentality. But really, all the time, he was probably thinking that we weren't even related. Maybe I had even been crowding him the way Uncle Mark crowded me. Maybe Corky didn't even really like me. But that was a crazy idea, I thought, shaking my head restlessly and turning over. One thing I could be sure of was that Corky liked me. It wasn't much, but it was something.

Everything was changed, though. If I were going to be friends with Corky now, it was going to have to be a more distant, proper sort of relationship. No more inviting myself for lunch any time I felt like it. No more showering at Aunt Myra's house. The thought of the shower embarrassed me because now that I thought it over in cold blood I realized that Corky had probably never thought of me as a cousin. He had almost said so. And friends didn't invite themselves to lunch and borrow your parents' shower.

I sighed. The problem was that here I was telling myself that I needed to put more distance between myself and Corky, when really, with things the way they were, I needed him more than ever. I needed somebody I could talk to, somebody I could depend on, somebody who knew what was bothering me. But now that everything was different between Corky and me, it was complicated and tricky. I didn't think I could sort it out until I was feeling stronger. Meanwhile, Aunt Myra's grass was just going to have to get taller and taller.

Suddenly I heard the phone in the family room. I struggled up from the couch and went to answer it.

"Fran? It's Steve."

I was surprised at how happy I was to hear his voice. There was nothing confusing about my relationship with Steve. Last week he had been just a boy I knew and this week he was still just a boy I knew. Totally simple.

"Oh, hi, Steve."

"Hey, I wonder if you'd like to try to catch the Early Bird Special with me at the movies tomorrow. I just found out they're doing a sneak preview of *War of the Galaxies*."

"That sounds super," I said, trying to infuse sweetness and docility into my voice. It occurred to me that maybe the reason my relationship with Steve was so simple was that it wasn't a relationship at all. It was like acting a part.

"The only problem," he said, "is that tomorrow I've got to work until six, which means we're going to have to cut it pretty close. Is there any way you could get out to the airport so we could leave together from there?"

It says something about my state of mind that I didn't even care that Steve was taking me for granted already on only our second date. So what if he was only giving me twenty-four hours notice and he expected me somehow to get all the way out to the airport to meet him? For the first time I understood the meaning of the saying, "Any port in a storm." I needed to get out of the house and get my mind off my troubles, and Steve was my escape.

"I could bicycle out there," I offered. "The airport's not much past Corky's family's farm and lots of times I've bicycled out that far."

"Bicycle?" Steve said, as a gardener might say, "Slugs?"

I realized that bicycling didn't fit with Steve's image of me. It probably didn't measure up to his standards of glamor. He would have preferred for me to arrive on horseback, in a small plane, or at least in a Ferrari. But since all I had was a bike, he was just going to have to put up with it.

"Well, all right," he said grudgingly. "Do you think you can get here by six?"

I assured him that I could. I realized though I was going to have start out way ahead of time and go very slowly, or else in this heat I would get all sweaty, which would do even more damage to Steve's image of me than my arriving on a bicycle.

Chapter Eight

The next afternoon I dredged up a pair of pink slacks and a ruffled blouse, which was the closest thing I could manage to a sweet bicycling costume, and I left with lots of time to spare to go meet Steve. I bicycled with exquisite slowness out of our neighborhood and down State Road 43, going toward the airport. Unfortunately, this route took me right past Corky's family's farm, but there was no cure for that since it was the only road that led directly to the airport.

As I drew up to the fences that marked the edge of the farm I began to feel singed, as if I were getting close to dry ice. I biked past the driveway to the stables and I saw Corky in the distance, standing by the stable. I was too far away to see the expression on his face, but the way he was standing holding the saddle in perfect quiet was eloquent. He was obviously paying close attention as I passed on my old red bicycle. I had already decided I was going to pretend not to hear him if he called to me, but when he didn't call, I felt ridiculously let down.

As I passed the farmhouse and headed on past more fences and in the direction of the airport I knew I was out of his sight, but still I cringed as if a gun were trained on my back. I was so anxious to get past the farm I almost overdid it on the speed. I had to force myself to slow down.

It seemed like forever, but at last I was bicycling decorously up to the airport. I saw its windsock full of wind and pointing east atop the humble little brick building that served as the airport offices, where Steve dispensed tickets and checked luggage. To the north was the broad runway, and around the edges of the airport were parked a lot of small airplanes belonging to private owners. In the distance I could make out the hangar where the commuter airline stored some planes.

I wheeled my bicycle in the front door of the terminal building. Steve looked out his ticket window. "You're not bringing that thing in here, are you?" he hissed.

"If I leave it outside, it could get stolen," I said.

He looked at the old bicycle with visible distaste. "Who would want it?" he said.

"You'd be surprised," I said.

Finally, he came out and helped me roll it to the back of the ticket counter and lean it against a filing cabinet. Glancing at the clock on the wall, I saw that I had allowed myself such a generous amount of time for the journey that in spite of how slowly I had gone, I had arrived a half hour early.

Steve went to the front door and looked out. I think he was hoping no one would show up wanting a ticket. He was probably worried that someone might think the awful old bicycle belonged to him. As he stood at the door the afternoon sun shone golden light on his face. I noticed with detached interest that his profile had completely lost its magic for me. I could certainly still see that he was good-looking, but it was like looking at a work of art in a museum. You could enjoy it without having to touch it or needing to have it for your own. I began to see with a strange clarity that I was going to drop Steve as soon as was decent. Corky had been right. There wasn't any point in having a romance with someone you didn't like.

"That's funny," Steve said, still looking out the door. "There's a plane parked over there that I don't recognize."

I looked out the door in the same direction and saw there was a plane there, all right. What I didn't understand was how you could recognize a plane. They all looked alike to me. I could tell this was just a little plane, not one of those jumbo jets. But I didn't see how you could tell it from all the other planes in the world. Steve went to get a broom from behind the counter.

"What are you doing?" I asked.

"I'm going to sweep out the plane," he said.

"Sweep it out?" Steve might not be my type, but he had never struck me before as an outright nut.

"I've never been inside one of those before," he said. "I'd like to look her over." I noticed his eyes had begun to glow with enthusiasm.

If I stayed in the terminal, I was afraid somebody might show up and expect me to sell them a ticket, so I trailed along behind him. He folded down the door of the plane and we mounted the steps that were built into it.

"That's funny," he said. "I've never seen anybody reinforce their steps like that."

"Reinforce their steps?" I peered closely at the metal steps and did manage to make out that steel plates had been riveted over the original steps. "This plane must be owned by somebody who really loves to pig out," I said.

Steve didn't hear me. He was stepping into the plane's dim interior. "Crikey," he said. "Look at that!"

I followed him into the plane expecting to see at least a pink elephant, which, when I came to think of it, would certainly explain the reinforced steps.

"The fuel line," Steve said. "You see, they've run a fuel line right into the passenger section."

"So what?" I said. It seemed like a good idea to me. That way you could refuel without landing.

"It's against FAA regulations, that's what," said Steve. "It's not safe. They're not supposed to unbolt the seats like that, either."

The more he said, the more I wanted to get out of that plane. It didn't seem to have struck Steve that the owner of this plane, having broken a few rules, might not want people poking around in his plane.

Steve began sweeping out the plane, while I peered nervously out one of its dusty windows, wondering what I would do if the owner showed up. I noticed a book of matches at my feet and bent to pick it up. It had a bright red cover and said, "Minnie's Motor Court." Somehow, I didn't expect that people who owned planes like this would stay at a place called Minnie's Motor Court. I looked at it curiously and stuck it into my pocket.

"Have you seen Corky lately?" Steve asked, his broom pausing for a minute.

Steve's question brought my mind back to my troubles with a jolt. "I saw him day before yesterday," I said. I realized suddenly that I wished Corky were with me right now. I missed him something fierce.

"Have you ever thought that he's kinda...unstable?" Steve asked.

"Never," I said. "Why do you say that?"

"Well, you won't believe this, but when I showed up this morning for my riding lesson he just looked at me and said, 'Buzz off, Blumenthal.' Don't you think that's weird?"

"I suppose he just wanted you to buzz off," I said.

"But it was time for my lesson. My regular lesson. And you know what he said? He said he had too much on his mind to bother with it."

I was more pleased than I wanted to let on to find out that Corky was upset. Maybe he was missing me the way I missed him.

"After all," said Steve, "he's not going to have much business if he treats people like that."

"I'm sure he's never done that before," I said.

Steve was back at his sweeping. "After that, I don't feel like going back there, I can tell you," he said.

"Of course not," I said. In spite of the warm glow of pleasure I felt at the thought that Corky was upset about the rift between us, I hadn't forgotten that the plane's owner might be back any minute. I wanted to get out of that plane. I peered out a window. "Steve," I said, "don't you think we'd better shove off? Maybe the owner of this plane doesn't want visitors."

Then I heard the creaking of the steps and realized that we were going to find out how the owner felt about visitors. Suddenly, a tall man's form was blocking most of the light from the open doorway.

"Well, well," he said.

I wasn't quite sure why that sounded sinister, but it did. The hair on the back of my neck tingled with fear. When the man stepped into the plane I could see he was wearing the kind of big, rimless sunglasses that celebrities wear when they're going incognito. He was smiling and had lots of white teeth, but somehow I felt absolutely sure the smile did not reach to his hidden eyes.

Steve, however, noticed nothing amiss. "Just sweeping her out for you, sir," he said.

"Fine," said the man. "That's just fine." He pulled a five-dollar bill out of his pocket and handed it to Steve.

"Thank you, sir!" said Steve.

"I wanted to get her spruced up," said the man. "I'm looking for a buyer for her."

"You're going to sell her?" said Steve.

"That's right. Let me know if you run into anybody who's interested."

I saw in a glance that Steve himself was interested and that if he could have put the five-dollar tip on it as a down payment he would have happily mortgaged his soul for the rest. There were stars in his eyes at the thought. I had noticed, however, that the owner did not give his name or any number at which he could be reached should Steve know of a buyer. I couldn't wait to get out of that plane. "It's six o'clock, Steve," I said uneasily. "Aren't we going to try to make that Early Bird Special at the movies?"

The man moved aside to let me out the door. I was relieved to realize that he didn't seem to count me as a person at all. Evidently to him I was just "the girlfriend," a nonentity. But I was sure his eyes followed Steve as we left the plane.

As we walked away from the plane I could hear the telephone ringing inside the terminal building. Steve sped up his walk to a trot and ran in to pick up the phone, tossing the broom into a corner as he went.

"Oh, hi, Ron," he said. "You're kidding me...well, okay...I don't see what else I can do...yeah, I'll tell Dad."

As he hung up the phone he announced gloomily, "That was Ron Watkins, my six o'clock relief."

It sank in on me that since Ron Watkins was on the other end of the phone and not in the room, it seemed reasonable to suppose that Steve's six o'clock relief was not coming.

"He says he's running a fever," said Steve.

"That's too bad."

"Yeah, I'm going to have to stay on here, at least until Dad gets back."

I thought that, considering I had bicycled miles into the boondocks only to be faced with bicycling back again, a few words about my sacrifice would have been nice, but that didn't seem to occur to Steve.

I went behind the counter to get my bicycle from beside the filing cabinet. I glanced at the door to make sure the plane's sinister owner wasn't in sight, then ventured a comment. "What did you think about all those changes they made on that plane?" I asked. "Wasn't that odd?"

Steve didn't seem to hear me. "Wouldn't you like to have a plane like that for your very own?" he said. "It's one sweet beauty." I could tell by his dreamy expression that the strings of his heart were playing "Off We Go into the Wild Blue Yonder." "A person who has a plane has some scope," he was saying wistfully. "If I had a plane, I could get my pilot's license in no time. I'd be in a good position to show what I could do, then."

I wheeled my bicycle out from behind the counter and headed out the front door. "I'd better go now," I said. "See you around, Steve."

He didn't seem to notice my departure. I hopped up on the bicycle and began to ride toward the gates. When I glanced back I saw that the plane's owner was just getting into his car. It was a long, sleek, shiny red car, but there was something odd about it— it had muddy license plates. I had never heard of a shiny car with muddy license plates. It didn't make sense. But there were a lot of things about that guy and his plane that didn't make sense.

The red car started up with a roar, did a sharp U-turn in front of the terminal building, and headed out the airport gates going much too fast as it passed me. With narrowed eyes, I watched it head down State Road 43. I didn't have the slightest doubt that the plane's owner was up to something.

Suddenly I began bicycling after him as fast as I could, the warm summer air whooshing past my ears as I sped along the highway. I hadn't made a conscious decision to follow the man, but I was really curious to see what he was up to.

He had a head start, but it wasn't long before I began catching up with him. He must have slowed down. I didn't want him to see I was following him, so I slowed down, too. He must have been going only fifteen or so miles an hour by then. It was pretty clear to me that he was looking for something.

We began coming up to Corky's family's farm. The fence of the north horse pasture was on my side of the road, and Devil stood there watching the red car as it passed him. On the other side of the road was Mr. Hennessey's soybean field. All at once, I saw what the man in the red car must have been looking for. Three cars were pulled off the road about fifty yards ahead of me, parked on the grass shoulder of Mr. Hennessey's field. The man in the red car pulled off the road there, too. Then he got out and walked over to the group of men standing near the cars. It looked as if the bunch of them had arranged a meeting.

The men were all wearing sunglasses and their cars were all the same type—long-hooded, shiny, and powerful-looking. I couldn't see the men very well. I was too far away. But I could see them well enough to make out that they were a slick type not commonly seen hanging around soybean fields. I began to be sure they were the drug smugglers Dad had read about.

It seemed to me that the strange alterations made to the little plane must have been made to enable it to transport some illicit cargo over a long distance without attracting official attention. The seats had probably been unbolted to make room for more cargo, and the fuel line must have run into the passenger section so they could fly from South America, say, to North Carolina without risking detection by stopping to refuel. I supposed the pilot of the suspicious plane must have had to jettison his illegal cargo for some reason, and now they were all trying to recover it. Nothing else made sense. If those guys out there were discussing soybeans, then I was Tinker Bell.

I didn't want to get too close to the men. In fact, I was beginning to feel as if the farther I got away from them, the better. I got off my bike as quietly as possible and pushed it behind a clump of trees by the pasture fence, jumping when a twig cracked under the bike's tires. I wasn't really hidden by the trees, but at least I didn't feel as if I were right out in the open.

I noticed that Devil, who was standing at the fence a few yards from me, was watching the men, too. He had always liked to stand by the road and look at cars as they went by. His flanks were satiny in the sunshine, and as I approached he turned his shapely head to look at me with large, liquid eyes. His ears moved alertly. I was glad to see that the men some fifty yards down on the other side of the road took no notice of him. It made me hope they weren't going to notice me, either. I was already wondering how I could get out of there without them seeing me. Now that I felt sure they were criminals, I wasn't too keen about hopping on my bike and riding past them.

The men seemed to be conferring. One of them pointed toward the soybean field, then they talked some more. I hoped they were planning to split up and search the field on foot. If they did that, I thought I had a good chance of slipping away unobserved. I promised myself that if I could get away without them noticing me, I would never play girl-detective again. I couldn't believe I had got myself in a dangerous spot like this after a lifetime of being so careful to preserve my skin. Never again, I said to myself.

Just then, one of the men caught sight of me. "Hey!" he shouted. He began striding toward me and another man came up behind him. My heart leapt up into my throat and began to pound wildly there. I knew I could never outrun those men on my bicycle. They had four fast cars. And all at once I knew I desperately wanted to outrun those men.

Devil, seeing the men walk purposefully toward us, gave out one of his awesome snorts. I eyed him uneasily and suddenly realized that I was more afraid of the men in dark glasses than I was of him. Almost before I realized what I was doing, I scrambled up the fence and jumped on his back, grabbing desperately at his mane. He shook his head and stamped, but I didn't slip off.

I remembered it was your legs that were supposed to hold you onto the horse, so I squeezed my legs like terrified parentheses tightly against his sides. I felt as if I were very high up—too high. I wished I had a seat belt. But casting a glance to one side, I saw that the men had already covered half of the distance in my direction and were breaking into a run. Holding my breath, I risked releasing the grip of my legs just enough to give Devil a sharp kick with my heels. He snorted, making a deep noise like the voice of doom. Then he took off running.

I held on to the hair of his mane with all my strength and squeezed my legs against him until they were numb. He cantered up a rise in the pasture, and in spite of my death grip, I felt myself slipping back until I was sure I must be going to slip off his hindquarters. Then suddenly he headed downhill, and I felt as if I were going to be pitched over his ears. But somehow, through it all, I managed to hold on, and mercifully the ground soon leveled out. The grass below his pounding hooves looked blurry and far, far away.

I was afraid to look behind me for fear I would lose my balance, but I didn't see how the men could possibly be following me. Already I must be out of their sight, now that I was past the rise in the pasture. They wouldn't even be able to tell in which direction I had gone.

If only I could stay on! I became dimly and uncomfortably aware of Devil's backbone and of the way his mane was cutting into my clutching fingers, but I was so terrified that none of that mattered much. I told myself I had always said I'd seen Corky give so many riding lessons, I could have given one myself. Now was my chance to prove it. The only problem was that none of the instructions I could remember seemed to apply now, when I had no saddle or bridle to hold on to. And every time I bounced or slipped a bit on Devil's back, I imagined myself falling under his legs, my skull caving in at the first blow of his hoof.

Suddenly I saw the stable. Devil seemed to be heading in that direction. He was running so fast it was like falling, and soon the stable yard was looming ahead of us. Then all at once I saw Corky. He had just come out of the stable. He stood frozen with astonishment, then started toward us. I was so glad to see him I almost lost my grip on Devil's mane in my relief. I had begun to wonder what would happen if Devil came to a sudden stop, but now I exhaled peacefully. Whatever happened, Corky would know what to do. He was just ahead of us, reassuringly familiar in his buff pants and his boots.

"Fran!" he yelled. "Are you nuts? What are you doing?"

Just then, Devil came to a full stop right in front of Corky, and as I had feared, I came tumbling down. It all happened so fast I wasn't sure exactly how it happened, but somehow Corky caught me.

"I've got to call the SBI," I panted, wriggling out of his arms. Unfortunately, when I struggled free and got my feet on the ground, my knees seemed to want to buckle. My legs were worn out from holding so hard on to Devil. But I knew I had to somehow get into the house and put the authorities on the trail of those characters.

Chapter Nine

I limped toward the house and up the back steps, Corky trailing after me. "What in the name of heaven is going on, Fran? Will you tell me that?" he asked.

"Lock the door," I said, as we went into the house. "I've got to call the SBI."

Corky looked as if he were bursting with relevant questions, but he did as I asked. I saw him pulling the bolt closed on the door. I grabbed at the phone and quickly dialed the number of the State Bureau of Investigation. "Ms Margaret Simmons, please," I said.

Luckily Ms Simmons, whom I remembered from the day she spoke at our assembly, was not out apprehending criminals. She came straight to the phone. I told her all about the suspicious plane, the sinister men, the soybean field, and everything. To my relief, she seemed to take me seriously.

"I'll send some people right out," she said. "Now let me confirm that location. You're at State Road 43, about a mile south of the Wessconnett Airport."

I shuddered at the thought of still being out there near those creepy men. "I'm not there anymore," I explained. "That's where I left the men. I'm at the Joseph Hayden farm, inside, with all the doors locked." I glanced nervously at the bolted door.

"Good," she said. "You stay right there. Now give me your number, in case I need to call you back."

When I finally hung up, I noticed Corky was looking at me in blank amazement. And no wonder. "Can I have a cold drink?" I said weakly. Now that I had notified the proper authorities I felt suddenly like collapsing, as if I were a balloon left over from last week's birthday party.

Corky went into the kitchen to get a drink while I took off my shoes and wiggled my toes and flexed my legs, trying to get some feeling back in them.

"Okay," he said when he came back in and handed me the drink. "I heard you telling those people the story. But what I don't see is why Steve let you go off following a bunch of suspected drug smugglers. He must have been out of his mind."

"He didn't know," I said. I explained how our date had to be called off and how I had followed the red car on the spur of the moment. "You know Steve," I said, "his head is full of dreams and glory. It didn't seem to strike him that there was something fishy about that plane. He knows all about planes, and he told me how this plane had broken all kinds of rules, but he just didn't seem to put two and two together. Maybe it's because I'm just more naturally suspicious, but all the time I kept wondering what it could all mean. I began to see that the people using that plane had fitted it out for some special, probably illegal purpose. So naturally I thought about the drug-smuggling ring Dad had been reading about in the paper the other night. Then one thing led to another."

"I get you," Corky said ironically. "Once you figured out that these guys must be desperate criminals, you naturally had to work out a way you could end up in their clutches."

"Okay," I admitted. "I wasn't too bright. I didn't think it all out before I followed that car. But at least I survived to tell the tale."

Corky grinned. "As long as I live," he said, "I'll never forget the sight of you galloping along bareback on Devil. Didn't I tell you he was a great horse?"

"I should be the one getting the praise," I said. "I'm the one who made the death-defying ride on that monster."

"You looked pretty good up there," he admitted.

I couldn't help limping over to the side window and nervously peering out.

"Do you really think those guys could have followed you?" said Corky. "They'd have to trail Devil over the grass. Did any of them look like trackers?"

I thought of the slick city suits and the celebrity sunglasses. "No," I said with some conviction. "I guess there isn't much chance of that, really. And maybe I frightened them. Maybe they just took off driving in all directions." I looked around me. "Where is everybody?" I asked.

"Mom and Dad went to the hospital to visit your mom. Then they're going out to dinner." He threw himself into Uncle Joe's leather chair, which gave a protesting creak. "I didn't feel like going," he said flatly.

There was an uncomfortable silence while I looked at the floor some. "I guess I've acted pretty awful," I said, tracing a pattern on the carpet with my toe. Now that I'd had a little while to get over the shock, I realized it wasn't fair to blame Corky for not telling me about my adoption. If our roles had been reversed, I wasn't sure I would have wanted to break that kind of news to him, either.

"I used to imagine how you were going to find out about being adopted," he said, "and I always thought things were going to be simpler then."

"Simpler, ha!" I said.

"For me, anyway," he said.

I took a deep breath. "It doesn't have to change anything," I said. "I'm all over being upset. I just won't tell Mom or Dad or Uncle Mark that I know and I'll just forget about it and everything can go back to the way it was.''

He didn't say anything, but I felt as if his silence spoke clearly.

"The only thing is," I went on lamely, "that I feel all different. Mom and Dad still feel like Mom and Dad to me because they raised me, but Uncle Mark really is my father and somehow that changes things right there. I can't help wanting to find out more about Sweetsie Face and what happened to her. And I don't see how I can find out without asking." I pawed at the carpet some more, then burst out, "And then, there's you, and you aren't even my cousin anymore."

"I hope you aren't going to go all teary about that," he said crossly. "Being related isn't the only thing that counts in the world, you know."

I got all teary about it anyway and sat down abruptly on the couch. "It's not the same," I said. "I don't feel like it's the same. Now when I think about how I kept saying you were like a brother to me and everything, it just embarrasses me. You should have told me. I feel so dumb.''

Corky lunged out of the chair and paced restlessly around the room, ending up gazing thoughtfully at the fireplace with his back to me. I looked at him standing there and thought what a dear, familiar back it was.

''Just because it's different,'' he said finally, ''doesn't mean it's worse.''

I sniffled. The strain of attempting to round up a ring of drug smugglers and riding wildly over hill and dale atop a fierce horse was beginning to tell on me. If a kitten had sneezed at me, I would probably have fallen flat on my face. I'm not up to an emotional scene like this, I thought. It wasn't fair for me to have to escape from a band of criminals only to have to hash all this out.

He wheeled around and faced me. ''I mean, there's nothing to stop us from dating, for example, just like anybody else.''

I was amazed to see he was turning red in the face. It was so totally unlike him to blush that I giggled a little. He wheeled around again and contemplated the fireplace. "Of course, if it hits you that way," he said in a muffled voice, "forget it."

I couldn't stand it that he had misunderstood me. I could hardly walk, my legs were so wobbly, but I managed to get up and totter over to him to put my arms around his waist. "I didn't mean that," I said. "It doesn't hit me any way but a nice way."

I was surprised at how comfortable I felt with my arms around him. I leaned my head against his back, resting my cheek against his shirt and smiled a little. It was a new sort of closeness, I thought. It was nice.

He turned around and gave me a hug. I was relieved to see that he looked happier and that he wasn't red in the face anymore. Everything was changing, I thought, but Corky was right. It didn't have to be worse.

Just then the phone rang and Corky bolted for it. It turned out to be for me.

"Fran? Margaret Simmons here. I thought you'd like to know that with the help of a police roadblock we were able to apprehend two of the suspects you put us on to. We gave chase to the other two but they managed to elude pursuit."

"They had fast cars," I said.

"We have men out now combing the soybean field for evidence," she said. "We've already called the airport, and we should be taking custody of the plane any minute."

I wondered what Steve had thought when he got word from the SBI that they were seizing his dream plane. He was probably totally flabbergasted.

After I hung up I filled Corky in on what Ms Simmons had told me. I would have liked to sit down and hold hands with Corky and look into his eyes and talk some more about him and me, but events were moving too fast for that. "I'd better get home," I said. "I want to tell Dad all about it before he hears it on the radio or something."

"I'll run you home," Corky said.

As we went out to the car I thrust my hands into the pockets of my pink slacks and felt the book of matches with my fingers. I fished it out and looked at it wonderingly—"Minnie's Motor Hotel" with names and phone numbers scrawled on the inside cover. "I think I'd better hand this over to the SBI," I said. "I picked it up on the floor of the plane. Maybe these names and phone numbers are going to turn out to be important.''

Corky slid into the car and I hopped in beside him. As we pulled out onto the main road, he chuckled a little. "Looks like you're going to be the chief witness for the prosecution," he said.

"What's funny about that?"

"I was just thinking how Steve is going to hate it," he said.

"You don't hate it, do you?"

"Why should I? I was always telling you you weren't a coward. This just shows I was right." He shook his head. "I'll never forget the sight of you galloping in on Devil," he said. "Never if I live a million years. I could make a decent rider out of you, you know."

"So you're always telling me. Maybe I'll give it a try."

"No kidding?" Then, as if he were afraid I'd change my mind, he added hastily, "You've got good balance. Natural form."

I knew this kind of encouragement was the sort of thing Corky fed to all the kids he taught riding to, but I couldn't help being pleased. The fact is, I had surprised myself with that hair-raising ride on Devil. I hadn't

realized I had it in me. I saw now there was
no reason why I shouldn't learn to ride.
Maybe Corky was right. Maybe I would end
up a real horsewoman.

I wondered how I had gotten in the habit
of saying no to so many things. It was funny
that I seemed to be afraid of being over-
whelmed by the strong personalities around
me. After all, I was a fairly strong person-
ality myself. That was something I was
starting to see. It was time I started opening
up to life more. Exploring a few possibilities. Maybe I would even go up to New
York and visit Uncle Mark. I didn't see how
else I would find out the answers to some of
the questions I had.

Who am I? I thought to myself watching
the fields fly by outside the window. Who
am I?

I hadn't realized I had spoken out loud
until Corky said, "You're Fran. Who else
could you be?"

"You know what I mean. I mean, who
am I really."

"You're the same person you were last
week. All this adoption business doesn't
change who you are."

"It changes everything," I said. It was hard to explain to Corky, who sat so securely between his two natural parents on his ancestral farm, but my ideas about who I was were changing. My feelings were slippery and hard to figure out, but I knew things were different. And I hadn't figured out yet where Uncle Mark fit into my life.

"What's wrong?" said Corky.

"I was wondering if, when Uncle Mark finds out I know all this stuff, he's going to go around telling all his friends that I'm his daughter," I said glumly.

Corky gave it some thought. "Well, your Uncle Mark doesn't strike me offhand as a very private kind of person."

"How right you are!" I said, overcome by awful visions of being paraded all over New York as "Mark's little girl." What if the story somehow leaked to *Personalities*? I shuddered.

"Remember, you're going to have to tell your folks before you tell your Uncle Mark or it's going to hurt their feelings."

"I know. But I'm not going to tell them for a while yet. Not until Mom's out of the hospital." The more I thought about it, the more I realized this was going to take the

kind of careful, large-scale planning that
went into the launching of the space shut-
tle. It was like a launching in another way,
too—it was a leap into the unknown. There
was no way of telling just how my life would
change once Uncle Mark and my parents
realized that I knew the truth.

Dad's car was in the driveway, so I knew
he was home. Corky walked with me up to
the door. As I was reaching in my pocket to
pull out my key, he put his arms around me
and looked at me, his eyebrows bent down.

"I love you, you know," he said
seriously.

I'm sure I must have turned white. If
Corky wanted revenge for me surprising
him in the kitchen the other day, with that
line about caring, he had it now. For a second, I felt as if I were going to pass out
from sheer shock.

He dropped his arms to his sides. "Well,
just thought I'd mention it," he said. Then
he got into his car and was gone.

I stood frozen to the spot, trying in my
confused way to sort everything out. Did he
mean he loved me like a sister? Or like Antony loved Cleopatra? I was going to have
clear that up one of these days.

Suddenly Dad opened the door and looked at me with puzzlement. "What are you standing there for, Fran? Did you lose your key?"

I caught a quick breath. "Uh, no," I said. "I've just been trying to figure out how to begin telling you about my day." As I stepped into the house I felt almost as if I'd never seen it before. "I can't think when I've had a more...interesting day," I said, a little dazed.

Chapter Ten

The next week Mom got out of the hospital, and a few days later I was featured in the newspaper—"Local Teenager Helps Bust Suspected Drug Ring." Dad bought ten copies of the paper and sent a clipping to Uncle Mark. The *Banner* had taken a pretty good picture of me, and they managed to spell my name right, too. I was pleased, but at the same time, I couldn't help feeling a little bit exposed. There's something awfully public about having your picture in the newspaper.

The funny thing was, though, after my picture was in the paper I felt braver. It was like in *The Wizard of Oz* when the wizard pins a medal on the cowardly lion's chest and the lion is suddenly convinced he's brave. When the *Banner* certified that I was a heroine, I started feeling as if they must be right.

As soon as Uncle Mark got the clipping he called up to congratulate me, and being Uncle Mark, he didn't wait until after five when the long distance rates go down.

"How about that!" he crowed. "You're famous. What put you on the track of those guys?"

I explained about meeting Steve at the airport and about how I had happened to see the inside of the plane with all its unusual modifications. It was a complicated tale, but Uncle Mark followed it with no trouble. I had never noticed before but he was quick on the uptake. You didn't have to cross every *t* and dot every *i* with him. The steps puzzled him, though. "Why reinforce the steps?" he said. "I don't get it."

I had wondered about that myself, but since I had had lunch with Ms Simmons, the SBI agent, I knew the answer. "The smugglers were in the habit of opening the plane's door while they were still up in the air," I explained. "Then they would throw the bales down to their contacts on the ground. The door and the steps had to be reinforced so they wouldn't get torn off when the wind was tearing at them and the bales were bouncing against them way up there in the air.''

He let out a low whistle, which I could understand. The idea of standing by an open airplane door and throwing something out didn't appeal to me at all. It was clear those guys would never have won the year's safety award.

"The SBI had the smugglers' regular drop strip staked out," I went on. "The pilot must have spotted the stakeout from the air and gotten scared because he flew past his regular drop spot and threw the bales out all over Mr. Hennessey's soybean field instead."

"And that's where you saw them?"

"Yup. They were meeting there to try to recover this stuff. I don't think they would have had much luck though, even if they hadn't been caught. When the SBI put out an appeal for help to the farmers, they started bringing in bales from four miles around. It wasn't what you'd call a pin-point drop."

"I can't believe you figured out what those guys were up to," Uncle Mark said admiringly.

"I'm a very suspicious person," I said.

He laughed.

I wasn't looking forward to letting Uncle Mark know I had found out the truth about my adoption. I could envision the scene too well. There I would stand, wanting a little simple information, while Uncle Mark would be emoting as if he were playing *Hamlet* for the Queen. He was too much of a ham to resist the dramatic possibilities of the long-lost daughter scene. And it was going to take some careful handling on my part to keep him from broadcasting the new development to every acquaintance and newspaper reporter from here to California. But I didn't see any way around it if I ever wanted to find out what happened to Frances Wostenholm Delacorte. And now that I was a heroine, I felt as if I could handle almost anything. Even that.

"I've been thinking I might take you up on that offer to visit you," I said suddenly, "if it's still open."

"What did you say?" he asked incredulously.

"I thought I might come up and see you," I repeated.

"I'd like that," he said, his voice sort of breaking.

It was pathetic, really. I felt like a heel. I supposed Uncle Mark had been standing on the sidelines all those years calling me up and sending me fancy presents in the hope of someday getting a kind word from me. I felt as if I'd been a pretty nasty little kid. I ought to have tried harder to be nice to him. It's not as if he were a criminal or something.

I had more or less quit worrying about him trying to take me away from Mom and Dad. I had decided that if he were going to try that, he would have done it years ago when he first got to be rich and famous. He must have figured I would be better off staying in Wessconnett with Mom and Dad, which, when I came to think of it, showed he had more sense than I had given him credit for.

At the other end of the line, Uncle Mark was getting lost in the excitement of planning what to do on my visit. He had started rattling off a list of things to do that would have taken a year to work your way through even if you were as fascinated with points of interest as a Baedeker guidebook and as full of stamina as King Kong. "What about the Statue of Liberty?" he inquired, as he began to wind down. "Do you want to see that? Or is it too touristy for you?"

"But I *will* be a tourist," I said.

"Sometimes you remind me so much," he said, getting choked up, "of...somebody I used to know."

I could guess who, so I was careful not to follow up on that remark. Then he seemed to decide he'd gotten too emotional because suddenly he started teasing me. "What's this about this fellow Steve you met at the airport?" he said. "I thought you told me there were no boys in your life."

"Steve isn't a boyfriend," I said. "Steve is ancient history. I saw him the other day and he ducked out of sight as if he owed me money. I think he doesn't like me being a heroine."

"Well, I love it, sweetheart," Uncle Mark said. "I just love it. I'm so proud of you."

After I hung up, Dad looked up from the game of solitaire he was playing and said, "I think that's the longest conversation you've ever had with Mark."

I shrugged. "He's not so bad," I said. "Oh, I'm not going to be in for supper. Corky and I are going to have a picnic over near the falls."

Dad covered his deuce with a three. "You're seeing an awful lot of Corky these days," he said.

"I've always seen a lot of Corky," I said. I wasn't really interested in going into how I felt about Corky. Especially when how I felt seemed to be changing. But I noticed that when Corky came by to pick me up, Dad looked at him closely. He had been under Dad's feet and raiding our refrigerator for years, but Dad was acting as if he'd never seen him before.

Corky noticed it, too. As we drove off he said, "Good grief, your dad looked at me for a minute there as if he thought I was after the family silver."

"He's not so dumb," I said.

Corky grinned.

It was really hot, even though it was getting to be suppertime, and Somerset Park, the big, wooded park near the falls, was mostly filled with families who were letting their small children run off steam. We carried our picnic basket past the tall, white Confederate monument, past the play equipment, and found a quiet place downstream from the falls to spread out our big, red-checked tablecloth.

I watched a cloud of gnats hovering over the water for a minute, then I stretched out and rested my head on Corky's legs. "It's too hot to do anything," I said. "What are we doing out here away from civilization and air-conditioning?''

"Enjoying the quiet," he said, lifting a strand of my hair and letting it fall.

Just then a five-year-old kid ran by in hot pursuit of another kid. "I gonna scalp you!" he screeched.

"No-o-o-o," wailed the proposed victim, putting on more speed. "Ma-ma!"

I giggled and struggled to get up. "We ought to eat some of this food," I said.

I pulled the paper plates out of the basket and put a couple of pieces of cold fried chicken on them. "I told Uncle Mark I'd go up to visit him next week," I said. "I decided there are some things I want to ask him."

"You're going to have to tell your parents you've found out," said Corky. "You can't keep putting it off."

I knew he was right. Mom was out of the hospital now and seemed fine. There was no reason to put off telling them any longer. Except that I wasn't exactly dying to face doing it. Now that things were back to normal at home, I wasn't keen to stir up another whirlwind of emotion.

I sighed. "This summer has turned out to be a lot more exciting than I thought it would be," I said. "In some ways I'm glad, but in some ways I'm just worn out with it all."

Corky reached into the picnic basket. "Have a pickle," he said, spearing one out of the bottle with a fork. It would have taken more than a temperature in the nineties to ruin Corky's appetite. He was already lighting into the chicken.

"I saw Steve the other day," I commented.

"What'd he have to say?" he said.

"Nothing. He dived into the ice cream shop the minute he caught sight of me."

Corky grinned. "Good old Steve, quick to rise to the occasion, the first to offer his congratulations and so on."

"You thought all along that I wouldn't much like Steve, didn't you?" I said.

"I was pretty sure," said Corky. "But there were some times you had me worried."

I looked upstream to the old textile mill where the falls, a curtain of water, fell straight and silvery to the lower level of the river. "Remember the time you tried to get me to go down the falls in a barrel?" I asked.

"I follow the association of ideas," said Corky, "but I don't think Steve was that bad. You should have taken me up on the falls offer, anyway. I didn't get too banged up, and it was one heck of a ride."

"Your barrel was a total loss," I pointed out.

Corky grinned. "It's still not too late, you know," he said. "I'd give you a second chance."

"No, thanks. Not for me. But, you know, I do think I am over being afraid of horses." Corky had already given me a few lessons, and I had been surprised to find that riding on Boss seemed too tame for me. I was ready for bigger things.

"Next time I'll put you on Black Watch," Corky said. "I think riding hunt seat would suit your style."

I knew that hunt seat was what people rode when they were jumping. And since Black Watch was a hunter, getting on in years, but still dependable over fences, I could put all that together with that gleam in Corky's eyes and see that he had big plans for me. But the idea didn't alarm me as much as I would have thought.

"Maybe it would be fun to learn to ride hunt seat," I said. I had come around to thinking that a little adventure wasn't necessarily a bad thing, taken in moderation.

"I'd better get one of those velvet hard hats," I added cautiously.

Corky took my hand and began to trace a pattern on it. "You don't have a thing to worry about. I see a long lifeline," he said. "And you see this little squiggly line here?"

I didn't believe in any of that stuff, but I found myself peering at the line he was tracing with his finger. "What's that?" I asked.

"You see how it touches your lifeline and goes right along beside it?"

All the lines looked pretty much alike to me, but I said, "Yes?"

"That's the Corky line," he said.

"You're making that up!" I said, pulling my hand away.

"Not completely," he said, smiling at me.

Take 4
Silhouette Romance novels FREE...

and get more great Silhouette Romance novels

—for a 15-day FREE examination—
delivered to your door every month!

In addition to your 4 FREE Silhouette Romance® novels—yours to keep even if you never buy a single additional book—you'll have the opportunity to preview 6 new books as soon as they are published.

Examine them in your home for 15 days FREE. When you decide to keep them, pay just $1.95 each, *with no shipping, handling, or other charges of any kind!*

Each month, you'll meet lively young heroines and share in their escapades, trials and triumphs... virile men you'll find as attractive and irresistible as the heroines do...and a colorful cast of supporting characters you'll feel you've always known.

Delivered right to your door will be heart-felt romance novels by the finest authors in the field, including Diana Palmer, Brittany Young, Rita Rainville, and many others.

You will also get absolutely FREE, a copy of the Silhouette Books Newsletter with every shipment. Each lively issue is filled with news about upcoming books, interviews with your favorite authors, even their favorite recipes.

When you take advantage of this offer, you'll be sure not to miss a single one of the wonderful reading adventures only Silhouette Romance novels can provide.

To get your 4 FREE books, fill out and return the coupon today!

This offer not available in Canada.

Silhouette Books, 120 Brighton Rd., P.O. Box 5084, Clifton, NJ 07015-5084

Clip and mail to: Silhouette Books, 120 Brighton Road, P.O. Box 5084, Clifton, NJ 07015-5084

YES. Please send me 4 Silhouette Romance novels FREE. Unless you hear from me after I receive them, send me six new Silhouette Romance novels to preview each month as soon as they are published. I understand you will bill me just $1.95 each (a total of $11.70) with no shipping, handling, or other charges of any kind. There is no minimum number of books that I must buy, and I can cancel at any time. The first 4 books are mine to keep.

BR28L6

Name _____ (please print)

Address _____ Apt. #

City _____ State _____ Zip

Terms and prices subject to change. Not available in Canada.
SILHOUETTE ROMANCE is a service mark and registered trademark.
SilR-SUB-2

First Love from Silhouette

COMING
NEXT MONTH

A CHANCE HERO
Ann Gabhart
When Shane dared to venture into the depths of the Chance
Woods he found something that changed his future, earned
him the respect of his dad and even helped him to win his first
girlfriend.

RIDING HIGH
Marilyn Youngblood
The wheel of fate had turned to bring Gabrielle and Angelo
on the same biking tour. Would they get their romance in gear
or were they riding for a fall?

BLUE RIBBON SUMMER
Nancy Morgan
Now that Lisa had achieved her heart's desire and had been
hired as a riding mistress at Cedar Lane Stables, she was
determined to let nothing cloud her success—not even
infuriating Jack Tyler.

ON THE LOOSE
Rose Bayner
Walter Humes would become a man of the world when he
visited France. He would speak the international language
with poise and ease. At least that had been the original idea.
Now he was beginning to wonder....

AVAILABLE THIS MONTH

JOURNEY'S END
Becky Stuart

FREE SPIRIT
Katrina West

SUGAR 'N' SPICE
Janice Harrell

THE OTHER LANGLEY GIRL
Joyce McGill